The Roman Villa

The Talisman - Book II

The Roman Villa

Michael Harling

vii

Lindenwald Press

To Mitch and Charlie
Without whom there would be no story.

Also by Michael Harling

The Postcards Trilogy
Postcards From Across the Pond
More Postcards From Across the Pond
Postcards From Ireland

The Talisman Series
The Magic Cloak

Finding Rachel Davenport

Chapter 1
July 2014

"Are you Mitch?"

"Yes."

"Mitch Wyman?"

"That's me?"

"Can you prove it?"

I looked up at the man. He was tall, taller than Dad, and his brown UPS uniform was two sizes too small. He had a cardboard box in one hand, a bulky tablet computer in the other and a frown on his face.

"I'm thirteen," I said, "I don't have a driving license or anything. Will a library card do?"

"Does it have your photo on it?"

"No."

The man consulted his computer screen. His frown deepened. "I'm not supposed to give this to anyone but Mitch or Charlie. Is Charlie at home?"

"Yes, but he's the same age as me and he doesn't even have a library card."

"Mitch," Mom called from inside the house, "who are you talking to?"

"That's my mom," I said. "She just called me Mitch. Is that good enough?"

The man shook his head. "Okay, but you need to sign." He held out the computer and I scrawled my name on it using the attached electronic pen. It looked nothing like my signature, but he handed me the package—which was the size of a tissue box—and, without a word, returned to his truck.

"What's this?"

Charlie came up beside me and pulled the box from my hand. I let him have it. I already knew what it was.

"Hey, that's Granddad's writing. It's to both of us, and … oh, no. Not again. I want nothing to do with this." He pressed the box back into my hands. "I don't care what it is."

"Oh, no," I said as he walked away, "doesn't really cut it." I felt suddenly weighed down, but also strangely relieved. A rising sense of dread had been with me since school let out, but then June ended, Independence Day came and went, baseball season was well under way, and I had begun to hope. I stood in the open doorway, feeling the early evening breeze, watching a full moon peek through the trees across the road. This was, I realize, what I had been waiting for.

"Who was at the door?" Mom asked from behind me. "And what's wrong with Charlie?"

"Delivery man," I said, holding the package up for her to see. "Present from Granddad. Maybe Charlie was hoping for something bigger."

She took the box. "From your grandfather?"

Her tone told me that she had been waiting too.

Granddad had sent us a present the year before, the strangest gift Charlie and I had ever received: a cloak. It was big—adult sized—heavy and made from an expensive-looking, blue velvet material. But that wasn't the strangest thing about it, the strange thing was what it did, which was send me and Charlie back in time, to England in the Middle Ages. That, of course, wasn't possible, so it had to have been a dream. That's what I told myself, but now that a second gift had arrived, the memories stirred and I remembered the mud and the smell and the pain and, even if it was a dream, it wasn't something I wanted to revisit.

And all this was made worse by Mom not being a fan of Granddad. Ever since he moved to England she's held a grudge, saying he abandoned us, and when he sent the first gift, she tried to keep it from us, which was why I wasn't surprised when she said, "I think I'll take this to your father. It may be something we wouldn't want you to have."

I followed her inside, to the living room. Dad was sitting on the couch, drinking a can of Foster's and watching *Bad Teacher*. He greeted us as we came in, but when he saw Mom and the package she was holding, his smile faded.

"Your father sent another gift to the boys," Mom said.

Dad put his beer on the coffee table, careful to set it on the coaster. "Well, that's nice. Isn't it?" He tried for a cheerful tone, but his words came out brittle, and he said them carefully, as if he was afraid they might break.

"That depends, what it is."

Dad gave a tight smile. "Well, it's certainly not a cloak."

Mom tore the box open and pulled out two small, leather sacks. One had an M embossed on it, the other a C. The bags made a 'chink' sound when she dropped them on the coffee table.

"What the …"

She upended the one with an M on it, which I took to mean, "Mitch," and a shower of silver coins spilled out, bouncing onto the table and carpet.

3

"Hey, those are mine," I said, kneeling to scoop up the coins.

"What?" Mom asked, dropping the empty bag. "You want to play with toy coins?"

"That's not the point," Charlie said, striding into the room. "Granddad sent them to us. They're ours." He snatched up the bag marked C and stepped back, folding his arms across his chest.

"Don't take that tone with me, young man," Mom said.

I dumped the remaining coins into the bag and pulled the draw strings.

"Was there anything else in the box?" Dad asked.

That distracted Mom. I moved away, standing next to Charlie.

Mom looked in the box. "Just this," she said, pulling out a piece of paper. Even before she unfolded it, I could tell it was written by Granddad.

I leaned forward, trying to see the writing. "What's it say?"

Mom turned away and scanned the letter. "Just the usual. How are you? Yadda, yadda, yadda. Went to the what-not shop. Old man. Yadda, yadda. Had these bags of coins. Thought you might find them interesting."

She stuffed the letter back into the box. "I don't think you should have them."

"Why not?" Charlie asked.

Mom glowered at him. "Don't you—"

"No," Dad said. "Don't you." He stood up and waved a hand in our direction. "Really, Donna, what is your problem? Just because my father sent them."

"That's not it."

Dad shook his head. "Yes, it is. Tell me, honestly, if

4

your father sent them this same gift, would you let them have it?"

Mom's face when white, then red. "That's … don't you …"

Charlie grabbed my arm. "C'mon, Mitch. Let's get out of here."

We went upstairs, into Charlie's room and sat on his bed. I was sure Mom would follow us, but she and Dad stayed in the living room, having a serious discussion.

"Do you think this means what I think it means?" I asked, staring at the leather bag in my hand.

"Yeah, it means Mom still has it in for Granddad. It's just like last year. I wasn't going to let her take that stupid cloak from us, and she's not taking these away, either."

"But the cloak. You know, what it did. And now Granddad has sent us these coins—"

"None of that means anything. We got the cloak. I had a dream. End of."

"But I had the same dream."

"So what? These coins? They're just toys. Another stupid gift from a clueless grandfather who still thinks we're six years old."

"And why would he think that? We were eleven the last time we saw him."

Charlie threw his hands in the air. "I don't know. Maybe he's going ga-ga. He is ancient, don't forget. He must be, what, almost a hundred by now."

"He's fifty-nine," I said.

"And that store he goes on about," Charlie continued, ignoring me. "He wants us to believe there is some sort of magical Wal-Mart over there that sells cloaks and fake coins. It's all in his head. And I'm not letting whatever it is get into mine." He tossed his bag

5

of coins at me. It bounced off my arm and landed on the bed. "You can have these. I don't want them."

I sat silent, staring at the small sack. I picked it up and shook it, listening to the chink of the coins. Then I dropped it back on the bed. He was probably right. Maybe. But still, I couldn't shake the feeling that the gifts were important.

"Don't you think we should at least try to use the cloak again?"

Charlie jumped off the bed and spun around to face me. "No," he said, clenching his fists. "That's ridiculous. You know we've tried. You know it's just a cloak. You know these are just toys."

"Look," I said. "I know you're scared. I'm scared too. But—"

"Scared? Of what? There's nothing to be scared of. Now you're talking like Mom, and I don't have time for either of you. Get out."

There was no sense talking to him. I wasn't sure what I was going to do but I knew there was nothing to be gained by staying there. I made a point of showing I wasn't angry, or frightened, by calmly standing up and walking into the hall.

"You forgot this," Charlie called after me.

I turned just in time for his bag of coins to hit me in the chest. It fell to the floor, spilling some of the coins. I scooped them up and went into my room. It was just after eight o'clock, and still light, but I didn't feel like doing anything, and yet I was too keyed up to sit still.

The television droned on down in the living room, so Mom and Dad must have finished their discussion. A few minutes later Charlie stamped down the stairs and went into the back yard. I put the bags of coins on my nightstand and tried to read, but I couldn't concentrate. A little later, Dad's car turned into the driveway. He must have gone out while Charlie and I were arguing. I looked out the window and saw him take a big box out of the back of the car and carry it into the house.

When the front door opened, Mom and Dad had a brief discussion, but it wasn't heated. Then there was nothing but the television. I was curious, but not enough to go downstairs. I stayed, kneeling in front of the window, watching the sky turn a deeper blue. The moon was higher now, well above the trees. I stared at it, blocking out the road, the power lines, the jet trails, imagining I was somewhere else in time. The thought frightened me, but also made me a little excited.

"What are you doing?"

The voice startled me, but I tried not to show it. I stood slowly and turned around. Mom was standing in my doorway and, behind her, was Dad, carrying the box.

"Just watching the moon," I said. "What's going on?"

"Your father and I have agreed," she said, stepping into the room, "that you can keep the coins, and the cloak."

"That's really good of you, seeing as how they belong to us," I said. In my mind. Out loud I just grunted and shrugged.

"I even got you a nice chest to put them in."

She went to my dresser and pushed all my stuff aside, not caring that I had is all neatly arranged. Dad came in behind her, holding the box, saying nothing.

The box was cheap and made of unfinished pine. I think it was a craft project that you were supposed to take home, sand smooth and paint, but they just plunked it on my dresser. It was about two feet wide, a foot and a half deep and had a rounded top, like a pirate's treasure chest. Something a six-year-old would be glad to have.

"They need to be kept safe," she continued, pulling open my bottom drawer. That was where I kept the cloak. It was too big to hang in the closet, so I'd folded it to fit in the drawer. Mom unfurled it and re-folded it so she could cram it in the box.

"There. That will keep it safe. It's what your grandfather would want." Her voice was high and slightly manic. I noticed she wasn't asking for my opinion. Dad said nothing. He just left the room and went back downstairs.

"Now where are those coin bags?"

There was no use arguing. I was just glad Charlie wasn't here because he wouldn't have handed them over the way I did.

"You have Charlie's too?" she asked, dropping them on top of the cloak.

"He didn't want his," I said.

Mom closed the lid and fixed the latch. "Well, that's fine." Then she pulled a small padlock out of her pocket and fastened it to the latch. "There, the gifts from your grandfather will remain safe now." She turned to face me. "You don't have a problem with that." It wasn't a question.

She left and I laid down on my bed, thinking. I hadn't gotten far when Charlie came in.

"What was that all about?"

I waved a hand toward the treasure chest. "Mom decided to lock up the cloak and the coins."

He gave a short laugh that sounded like a snort. "At

last, she's done something I agree with."

He returned to his room, leaving me to stare at the ceiling, something I decided I could do later. I went to the living room, where *Crimetime* was just starting. Mom seemed calmer and she even made popcorn as a way of apologizing for being such a bitch. Charlie even made an appearance and we all sat together watching TV like a normal, happy family.

At ten o'clock some news program came on, which Charlie declared was too boring, so he left. Half an hour later it became too boring for me, so I left too.

It was only 10:30, but Charlie was already in bed, apparently asleep, or at least not eager to talk to me. I put on my pyjamas and laid on the bed, watching the square of light coming through the window, cast by the glow of the moon, listening to the faint babbling of the television, and feeling the pounding of my heart.

I drew a breath and let it our slowly, trying to calm myself, recalling a line from a movie I had seen a long time ago: "You have the strength that comes from knowing." And I suddenly knew a great deal.

The first time we used the cloak had been an accident, and when it was over, neither Charlie nor I understood how or why it had happened. We remembered the adventure, however, and in the weeks that followed had tried various—though ultimately unsuccessful—ways of using the cloak again. But as the new school year approached, the memories faded, and we lost interest. So, I tucked the cloak away, and Charlie and I, and Mom, had forgotten about it.

But then the coins arrived.

Just seeing the package brought it all back—the stench, the pain, the fear, but also the joy of triumph—and when the box was placed in my hand, I knew why the cloak hadn't worked a second time, and I knew how we could, and should, use it again. I knew the danger we'd faced had been real, but I also knew it was important. I knew another trial waited, and I knew Charlie had to come with me, whether he wanted to or not.

All those thoughts had flashed through my mind as I'd held the package, and now, in the quiet of my room, they solidified into an unwanted certainty: I knew we had to go, and I knew we would, because I knew how to get the cloak out of the box.

Chapter 2

I had a lot to think about, and a lot of time to think it, while waiting for the house to fall asleep.

The television seemed to grow louder as the house grew quieter. Then, finally, it was switched off. The stairs creaked. I heard Mom check on Charlie, then I pretended to be asleep when she checked on me. The bathroom light went on, then off, and the house settled into silence.

What was Granddad up to? The bags seemed to be real leather, but the coins were fake—cheap, tinny replicas of Roman money. So, what did that mean? Were we going to go to Rome? I knew a bit about the Roman Empire from studying it in school, and from books I'd read, but not enough to prepare for a visit. I had thought we'd be going to England, because that was where we had gone last time. And it was where Granddad had—suddenly and inexplicably—moved to.

I had to admit it was odd, but I agreed with Dad that it was his life, and he could do as he pleased with it. Still, I understood why Mom was angry. Granddad had been a big part of our family, and then he just disappeared. That had been two summers ago, and I still missed him. I think Mom did too, though she turned her sadness into anger. But—and Charlie was right about this—that didn't give her the right to take it out on us.

It all fell apart when our great-granddad, Melvin, died. I couldn't be sad about that because I'd never met the man. He had moved to Canada before I was born. Dad told me I had met him once, but I was only two months old at the time. We'd travelled up to celebrate the 100th birthday of some relative of Dad's who had been born in England, and Great-Granddad Melvin had been at the party. This was why I didn't find Granddad's behaviour as odd as Mom did. His family came from England; why shouldn't he move back?

Apparently, Great-Granddad had moved to Canada after he retired, to be with that branch of the family, and when he died, Granddad had to go up to settle his estate. That's when he suddenly sold his business, and his house, and moved to England. He kept in touch, but never gave us a means of contacting him, so, yeah, I agreed with Mom on that; it was a bit crazy. And then, a year later, the cloak arrived.

I opened my eyes and realized I had been half asleep. My bedside clock read 3:15, so maybe I had been fully asleep. I listened. Silence.

Slowly, quietly, I dressed in jeans and a tee shirt. Then I put a light jacket on. I didn't know what the weather was going to be where we ended up and I wanted to be prepared. When I was ready, I picked up the chest, put it on my bed and turned it around. Then I used the screwdriver on my Swiss-Army knife to take the hinges off.

With the top flipped open, I took out the two bags of coins and the cloak. That was the easy part. Now I had to get Charlie involved.

I went to his room, tiptoeing quietly in my sneakers. Charlie was sound asleep, half-covered by a sheet, wearing a pair of shorts and an old Star Wars shirt of Dad's that had Luke Skywalker on the front and Darth Vader on the back. I felt bad about taking him on another trip (kidnapping was what he would likely call it) wearing that, but if I woke him up so he could change, we would never go.

We had never figured out why the cloak had worked that first time, but during the past year, at some point, I had learned that Morpheus was the god of sleep and dreams, and when I touched the package and the memories came back, I recalled the verse written on the scroll that had been with the cloak. It had said we needed to take Morpheus's hand. We had been knocked out, which is sorta like being asleep, while under the cloak, and that was what did it. So, all I had to do was get Charlie under the cloak with me and fall asleep.

I laid half the cloak over Charlie as carefully as I could, holding my breath until I was sure he was still asleep. Then I took a pair of his sneakers—hoping they would come along with us—and laid down next to him. I put the bags of coins on my chest, along with his sneakers, pulled the cloak over me, and waited.

Closing my eyes, I took a deep breath and let it out slowly, counting backward from ten, breathing in, and out, in and out, until I felt myself falling into a deep, dark pit.

Chapter 3
June 275 AD

The cloak whipped away. Sunlight blinded me.

"What the—?" Charlie's voice.

Then someone punched me.

"You asshole!" Charlie again.

A kick to my side, but it didn't hurt because whoever kicked me had bare feet.

I rolled away and got to my knees in time to see Charlie barrelling toward me. "I'm going to kill you."

I dove at him and grabbed him around the middle, knocking us both to the ground, Charlie flailing and shouting and me trying to hold him still and shut him up.

"I can't believe you did this."

"Quiet," I said. "We don't know where we are or who might be nearby."

"We're in some stinking, ancient wilderness. Just like last time."

"No. The coins. They were Roman. We must be in Rome. Or somewhere in the Empire."

Charlie stopped struggling, but I still didn't let him go. "The Roman Empire was pretty big," he said, "so that could be anywhere. And we don't know when we are."

I eased my grip and he pushed me off him, but he didn't try to hit me again.

"No matter where or when we are," he said, "I'm here dressed in pyjamas, with no shoes." Then he gave me a sharp punch to the arm.

"Ow! Hey. I did bring your sneakers."

The cloak was lying in a heap nearby, and next to it was one of Charlie's sneakers, but I couldn't see the other one, or the bags of coins. We scrabbled through the grass until we found them, and while Charlie put his sneakers on, I stuffed the coin bags into my pockets. They seemed bigger now and I had trouble fitting them in. I pulled one out and dumped a few coins into my hand. They didn't sound tinny and cheap like they had before. Instead, they gave a melodic clink, and they appeared more substantial.

"The coins," I said. "They've become real."

"Great," Charlie said as he stood and looked at his outfit with an expression of disgust. "We're rich. But we're still lost in a forest with no place to spend it."

I looked around. Like Charlie, I had thought we were in the woods because we were surrounded by trees. But these trees were all the same height and shape, and they were in straight rows, with strips of ankle-high grass running between them. The sky was clear, and a low sun shone through the leaves, casting dappled shadows. The air smelled fresh and carried the scent of morning.

"It's an orchard," I said. "These are apple trees."

"Okay, we've seen Roman apple trees. Now take me home."

I put the bag back in my pocket and made sure the coins were secure. "Um, I can't. Not right now."

Charlie shook his head. "You obviously figured out how the cloak works. Now get us back home." Then his face went white. "You do know how to, don't you?

15

If we're trapped—"

"We're fine," I said. "Yeah, I know how to get us back. But we can't do it right now."

"Why not?"

I considered explaining Morpheus to him, but I wasn't sure he'd want to hear it. "You have to be asleep. Do you feel like sleeping?"

"I feel like knocking your head off," he said, "and if I thought it would get me back home, I'd do it." He sat heavily on the grass. "So, we need to find a place to hide and wait until we get tired?"

"No," I said. "We need to stay here until we get tired. Don't you remember? The cloak only works if we're in the spot where we appeared."

Charlie shook his head. "In that case, we'll just sit here until we get tired."

I shrugged. There was no use arguing, and I couldn't think of anything better to do. I didn't know much about Rome, where we were, why we were here, or how much the money in my pocket was worth. The truth was, I only wanted to see if the cloak would work again. I hadn't planned anything beyond that.

I sat down, far enough away from Charlie where he couldn't hit me. "We might be here a while."

"So? There's no place we need to be. There's nothing stopping us from sitting here all day. And all night, for that matter."

I nodded, feeling a little foolish for bringing us both here, wherever here was. In the darkness of my room, it had seemed important, but now, killing time in an orchard for no good reason, it seemed a little crazy. I settled myself in for a long wait. Then I heard voices.

They were too far away at first to make out what they were saying, then they drew closer and, very quickly, closer still.

"Are you sure?" one of the voices asked.

"Yes," another answered. "Here, in this orchard. They were arguing. Maybe fighting."

"We should be careful. They may be raiders. Should we get Lucius?"

The owners of the voices came very near, and I saw them moving through the trees several rows away. They were men, dressed in tunics and wearing floppy straw hats. One carried a spear. And they were coming our way.

"We need to get out of here," I whispered to Charlie.

"To where?" He tried to sound casual, but he was already up, crouching, and ready to run.

"I don't know," I said, grabbing the cloak and folding it into a bundle, "but we have to go. Now."

"And how will we find our way back?"

I thought for a second. "Remember Pendragon? He used a rock to mark a trail."

Charlie felt around in the grass and came up with a small rock.

"It will have to do," I said. "Mark that tree, the one we appeared next to. And then mark some others as we sneak away."

Charlie struck at the tree with the rock. It wasn't sharp but after a few tries he skinned enough bark off the trunk to leave a mark.

"Let's go," I said. "This way. Slow and quiet."

Then someone shouted, "You there! Stay where you are."

Charlie dropped the rock, and I almost dropped the cloak, as we bolted down the row of trees. Behind us, the men shouted.

17

"This way," Charlie said, running into the trees.

I followed. It was harder going but better cover. Charlie zigged and zagged and I did my best to keep up, slapping branches out of my way as I ran. Behind us, the voices continued shouting, and there seemed to be more of them. What had we stumbled into? Was this some sort of secret army base? Were they soldiers or security guards? Whoever they were, they were armed and after us and that was a good enough reason to keep running.

"There's a clearing over there," Charlie said.

We raced toward it, dodging through the trees. When we got to the clearing, we both stopped. It was a road. Not a big road, just a track, but it was hard-packed, smooth and had ditches on either side. We would make good time on it. But then the shouts grew closer, and we realized our pursuers would too. Across the road was another orchard. We ran into that.

The men reached the road and paused. We stopped, trying to quiet our breathing, and laid down in the grass, keeping still, watching. There were four of them now, and they seemed to be having the same debate as we had about which way to go, only they had more time to discuss it. Charlie and I backed away, keeping low and silent. One man ran up the road, the other down it. The man with the spear, and his friend, came into the orchard. We tried to move quietly and keep out of sight, but they spotted us immediately.

"I see you," the man shouted. "Stand and show yourselves."

We decided to not take that advice and ran on, diving under branches and dodging around the trees. We had the advantage—being smaller and wearing sneakers—but still they gained on us. Their advantage was they didn't seem to be getting tired, whereas I was already winded. I couldn't run forever, and they didn't seem ready to give up.

Abruptly, the orchard ended. Running along its border was a low stone wall, and behind that was a forest. We vaulted the wall and ran into the woods. It wasn't a big forest, but it was thick with brush and brambles, and we didn't have to go far to be out of sight. Seconds later the men came to the wall, where they stopped. We crouched in the brush, keeping still, trying to hold our breath. The men stood next to the wall, looking our way but, for once, they didn't spot us. The taller, skinny man leaned his spear against the wall and folded his arms across his chest. I realized the spear was not a spear at all, but just a pole with a curved saw at the end. They weren't soldiers, they were farmers. Although, for the moment, they were no less dangerous. I wanted to tell Charlie what I was thinking, but I didn't dare move or even whisper.

"They are in the wood," the taller one said.

The other nodded. "They may have friends in there."

"If they are raiders," the taller one said as he picked up his saw, "the two of us will be no match for them. We must tell Lucius."

They left then, but they didn't go back into the orchard. Instead, they followed a path next to the wall. I waited until they were well out of sight before I spoke.

"I think we're safe for now."

Charlie brushed a twig out of his hair. "Yeah, but what do we do now?"

"We could wait here until dark."

"No, they're not going to let this go. They know

we're in here. What if that Lucius guy comes back with an army? We need to find someplace else."

He was right, but where could we go?

"Those guys went that way," I said, "so let's go this way."

"Get further back in the trees first," Charlie said, working his way out of the brush.

I followed, keeping low, trying to make as little noise as possible. When we were a good distance from the road, we turned and headed in a different direction. It wasn't long before we came to another wall. Beyond it was a dirt road and beyond that a field. Low, leafy plants grew in neat rows, allowing me to see to the other side, into another large field.

Men with hoes worked between the rows. Carts, pulled by donkeys or small horses moved through the fields and on the roads. The men were all dressed like the ones who had chased us—in loose tunics cinched at the waist with a belt of rope or leather. Some of the men were close enough for us to hear the chink of their hoes hitting the dirt, so we moved into the brush to better conceal ourselves.

"It's a farm," I said, unrolling the cloak so I could brush the leaves out of it. "A big farm."

"No shit," Charlie said.

To our right was the orchard, behind us, the forest, and in front of us, a field with no cover. There was no need for discussion. Keeping well back from the field, we turned to our left and, in a short time, came to a stream. We thought it might be the edge of the farm, but after wading across it we found a narrow strip of woodland and another, even larger field.

Charlie placed his fists on his hips. "This place goes on forever."

"It can't," I said. "If we just keep going, we'll get out of it at some point."

"Yeah, but how will we find our way back?"

"We've been going in a zig-zag pattern but always in the same direction. If we keep going that way, we can just retrace our route later, when it gets dark."

I didn't wait for him to agree. There was a path next to the stream and I went to that, following it in the same direction we had been going in. The good news was, if we found the stream again, we could find the forest, and from there we could find our orchard.

"Don't forget," Charlie said, coming up behind me, "there's no streetlights in the past."

I was glad he was behind me so he couldn't see the look on my face. I had forgotten about that. Wherever we ended up, once night came, it would be too dark to move.

Chapter 4

We walked in silence after that. Soon, the stream left the woods and meandered between two fields, each with men working in them. We crawled from bush to bush to keep out of sight, though occasionally the stream bed fell far enough below ground level that we could duck-walk through the gully and remain hidden, as long as we didn't make a lot of noise splashing in the water.

At the far end of the fields was another road, with a stone bridge arching over the stream. We climbed onto the road and turned left. Somehow, we would need to retrace our steps back to the stream, then past the fields to the orchards. It might have been easy except that we were still going further away, and getting back from wherever we ended up wasn't going to be easy. We'd have to stay awake all night, until the early hours of dawn, where we could see well enough to find our way. But this being a farm meant that even in those early hours, other people might be up and out doing chores.

I didn't mention this to Charlie. I just wished I had thought about it before I brought us here. I had been so excited about seeing if the cloak would work again, I hadn't stopped to remember that I didn't want to be here, either.

"What are we going to do?" Charlie asked. "There's no place to hide."

"If we stay on the road," I said, "we'll look less obvious. Just try to act normal and hope that those guys looking for us haven't come this far."

We continued on the road, walking briskly but not so fast as to cause alarm.

"How 'less obvious' can I look wearing this," Charlie said, indicating his pyjamas.

"Just do the best you can," I said, and kept walking.

There were about a dozen men working in the fields we passed, but only a few of them looked up at us and none of them shouted for us to stop. I felt my heart pounding harder and harder the longer we were exposed, but the road was straight and flat, so we made good time, passing each field in less than a minute and giving the farmers little time to become curious.

Then we came to a crossroad.

The road was wider than the one we were on, and paved with flat stones, but following it would mean turning again and I didn't want to make it harder for us to find our way back. So, we went straight.

We regretted it almost immediately. Along the path—for that was what the road had turned into— stood a row of stone houses. They were single story, with slanted, slate roofs, window openings and wooden doors. They were close together, and each had a low stone wall surrounding a small front yard. The grass here was tall but not wild, and there were few bushes and no brambles, which made me wonder if the people living there mowed their lawns.

Smoke rose from chimneys in a few of the houses and, as we stood wondering what to do, a woman emerged through one of the doors. She glanced our way but didn't seem alarmed. All she did was gather an armful of wood from a pile stacked in the yard and carry it into the house.

Charlie stepped behind a small bush. It didn't hide him; it only made him look like he was casing the place. "What is this?"

"I don't know," I said. "A town, or village, maybe."

"We shouldn't be here. Someone will see us."

He was right, but the path followed a creek and further on, there were trees, and the thought of cover was too tempting to ignore.

"If we just keep walking like we belong here," I said, "we should be okay."

"Not if they see me dressed like this."

"Well, I don't exactly blend in, either."

In the end, we unfolded the cloak and Charlie wrapped it around himself. It looked ridiculous, but it wasn't as startling as his pyjamas.

"Just keep walking," I said, "and if anyone comes out, don't make eye contact."

When we started walking again, I kept Charlie between me and the houses, figuring he'd look less out of place than I would. We passed three houses, then six. I made myself look away in case someone came outside, and looked toward the creek, instead. Then a strange feeling came over me, causing me to stop.

"This feels familiar."

Charlie turned my way. "How could it? Come on, we gotta get out of here."

I started walking again, slowly, glancing at the houses as we passed.

"The creek, this path, and those houses. They were just foundations the last time we were here."

"What are you talking about."

"This is the way to Pendragon's house."

This time, Charlie stopped. "You're talking crazy.

We're somewhere in Rome."

I looked at the house we were in front of, then moved on to look at the next one. And the next one. Then I froze.

"This is it. This is his house."

"How can it be?" Charlie said, an edge of panic in his voice.

I left him on the path and went to the house. A stone walkway led from a gap in the wall to the wooden door.

"Get back here," Charlie said, running to me and grabbing my arm.

I shook him off and stood in front of the door. It was made of oak planks and fastened to the wooden frame with big metal hinges. I pointed to a spot near the top. "Look."

"At what?"

"That's the knot in the wood. The place where Garberend had me carve an airplane."

"That's insane, and you're insane."

"No, this has got to mean something."

"Yeah, it means we're going to get caught if you don't move."

The door was open a little. I looked through the crack. "It seems empty." I took hold of the handle and pulled it open a little more.

"We are not going in there," Charlie said.

The interior wasn't as dark as I thought it would be. There didn't appear to be anyone inside, but Charlie was right, even if this was Pendragon's house, it was too dangerous to stay here. I eased the door closed. "Let's go, then," I said.

We'd only taken a few steps when we heard voices. Back toward the road, the woman who had come out to gather wood was outside again and talking to two men. The men were waving their hands and pointing in the direction we had come from, and one of the men, the taller and skinnier of the two, was carrying something that looked like a spear. They no longer wore their floppy hats, but I was sure I knew who they were.

"It's the two guys who chased us," I said. "We need to hide."

I pulled the door to the house open and rushed inside, followed by Charlie.

"Do you think they saw us?" Charlie asked, pulling the door closed.

"No. If they had, they'd be shouting and running this way. I think we're safe in here for the moment."

Charlie looked around. "Yeah, but where is here?"

I was certain it was Pendragon's house, or what would become Pendragon's house., which was why I was surprised by how light it was. When we had last seen it, the single window was covered by a shutter, the walls were dark, and the whole room had been filled with smoke from a fire burning in the middle of the floor. But this room had two windows, each covered with a gauze-like material that let in the sun. The walls were smooth, white and had colourful tapestries hanging on them. There was furniture too. A table and chair stood by one wall, and a bed was pushed up against the other. There were shelves and cabinets and something that looked like a dresser, all sitting on a tiled floor. The air inside was warm and held a faint whiff of smoke.

Charlie walked around the room, gazing up at the peaked ceiling. "What is this place?"

I went to the bed. It was narrow, but sturdy, and

made of wood, with blue and white striped blankets folded neatly over a mattress. There was even a plump pillow covered in the same material. All the furniture had a well-used look, but the room felt strangely modern. A TV sitting on one of the chests wouldn't have seemed out of place.

Charlie lifted the lid on a big, wooden box. "Clothes," he said, pulling out a handful of multicoloured material. He looked at it with disgust, dropped it back in the box and slammed the lid. "Girl clothes."

I looked around the room. "Someone lives here." Built into the wall near the bed was a small fireplace with a few glowing embers in it, and on a nearby shelf sat a sort of flattened teakettle made of clay. A wick stuck out of the spout, and it was burning, adding more light to the room. "And whoever it is won't be gone for long."

Then I heard a voice, shocked and angry. "What are you doing in my house?"

Chapter 5

It was a young woman, a girl, really, hardly older than we were and just a little taller. Like the woman we had seen, she wore a loose dress with a belt, but her dress looked cleaner, and her belt was a thick braid of coloured cords. Her red hair was tied back, and her green eyes glowed with anger, showing not a bit of fear.

"Thieves," she shouted.

Charlie pulled the cloak around himself and stepped away from the box. I moved back to be with him, facing the girl, my hands in front of me, palms out. "We're not thieves. And we're not going to hurt you."

"By the gods, you are right about that."

She started looking around. I had the feeling she was searching for a weapon. There was a broom and a metal poker next to the fireplace and I was glad we were closer to it than she was. Then she grabbed a ceramic jar off a shelf and raised her arm to throw it.

"Don't," Charlie said.

"Then get out."

We both hesitated.

She smiled in a way that didn't make her look friendly; she looked like she was gloating. "You're the ones they're looking for, aren't you?"

"Please," I said. "They've got it wrong. We're not thieves, or raiders, we're just lost."

"You managed to find your way into my house."

"Just let us go," Charlie said. "We don't want any trouble."

She lowered her arm. "Go where? Dressed like that, you'll find trouble wherever you go."

"We'll take our chances," I said. "Just let us go."

The girl shook her head. "I'm doing you a favour."

Then she turned to the open door and shouted through it. "Titus, Cassius, they are here."

"Don't," Charlie said. Then he looked at the floor and shook his head as the sound of running feet approached. "Oh man, this sucks."

I wanted to tell him I was sorry, but I didn't have time. The two men who had been chasing us rushed through the door.

"Are you hurt, Kayla?" the tall one with the saw that looked like a spear asked.

She shook her head. "No, Titus, they are not strong enough to hurt me, and they have no weapon. I found them in here, pilfering. They are vagabonds."

"Thieves," the other man, who must have been Cassius, said. He had a stocky build and dark hair, unlike his taller, thinner companion.

"No, we're just lost," I said.

They didn't listen. Cassius grabbed me by an arm and yanked me forward while Titus pointed his saw at Charlie. Charlie pulled the cloak tighter around him. "No need for that. We'll come quietly."

They marched us into the yard, me being pulled by the arm and Charlie with the saw poking him in the back. Kayla came with them.

"Should we bind them?" the tall one asked.

"You could," Kayla said. "But they won't try to escape. Where are they going to run to?"

Cassius let go, but his narrow eyes carried a threat.

29

Kayla pushed me from behind. "Move."

"To where?"

"The villa. Lucius will decide what to do with you."

We walked on, back the way we came. This time, a number of women came out of the houses to watch. We continued in silence until we got to the crossroads and turned toward the bridge. I found it odd that Kayla seemed to be in charge, when Cassius was the strongest and Titus had the only weapon.

"What is his condition?" she asked, waving a hand toward Charlie. "Does he not have any clothing on?"

Charlie glared at her. "I'm dressed. I just like this near me."

"I can see why," Titus said from behind us. "A garment as valuable as that would quickly be stolen away, just as you stole it from someone else."

"I didn't steal it" Charlie said. "It belongs to us."

Kayla looked at me. "How can a cloak belong to you both."

"Easy," I said. "Our grandfather gave it to us, to share."

"You are brothers?" Kayla asked.

I nodded.

"You have a rich grandfather who gives such expensive gifts," Cassius said, with a hint of envy in his voice.

"You mean a poor grandfather," Kayla responded without turning to face him, "who gives two boys a single cloak."

"I'm sure Lucius will appreciate it," Titus said.

My stomach tightened. Charlie walked with his head down, watching the road. Neither of us said anything.

We crossed the bridge and soon came to another crossroad. To one side, an unpaved road ran between a collection of houses. The houses were ramshackle and random, all different sizes and styles, unlike the row of houses we had found near the creek. Some were made of stone, some of wood and others from a combination of the two. The road was hard-packed but rutted and several people were out, carrying bundles of wood, or sacks, or live animals. One—a small girl—carried a flapping, squawking chicken into one of the houses. Their clothing was similar to what our captors wore, except the material looked thicker and darker, though that could have been from all the mud. To the other side there were no houses, just more fields and woodlands.

We went toward the fields on a road that grew wide and flat, covered in worn paving stones. Occasional carts and horses passed us, and a few people on foot. No one took much notice of us, and I tried to not take notice of them. What I did take notice of was the smell. As we'd approached the crossroad, a strong animal scent filled the air, a smell that had been absent while we'd been in the orchards and fields. Here, it was suddenly pungent, and we had to walk carefully around what was making it so pungent.

The road, if not the scenery, began to look familiar. If we were in the same place as last time, then the collection of houses behind us would be the village of Horsham, and we would be on the road Pendragon had taken us down, only now it was in better shape, and the forests and tangles of brush lining the sides of the road were cultivated fields. It looked miles more advanced, even though it had to be hundreds of years earlier, which didn't make any sense.

Even so, I was sure we were on the same road. All the details from our last visit—the people we had met, the skills we had learned, the sights, the smells—returned as if we had only just experienced them. That had probably happened as soon as we woke up, but I wasn't realizing it until now. I wondered if Charlie felt the same way, but he was still shuffling with his head down, as if he had given up all hope, which wasn't like him. It made me feel worse about getting him involved.

We walked on, in the opposite direction we had walked with Pendragon a year ago. I recalled we had crossed a small bridge with a stream running under it, and shortly after that we had passed a thicket where we had seen glimpses of an old ruin. If my calculations were correct, we would be coming to it shortly.

"Do you recognize this?" I asked Charlie.

Charlie grunted but didn't look up. Then the hedge bordering the road ended, revealing a paved driveway leading to the biggest house I had ever seen. It was made of concrete, painted white and topped with a peaked roof covered in orange tiles. It was laid out in a huge square, with an upper story on one side, and a porch—held up by thick columns—that ran around the entire structure.

"That's what I saw," I said, unable to stop myself. "Those columns. They were the ruins in the woods, where Pendragon told us the giants had lived."

Charlie glanced up. His eyes got big for a second, then he looked back at the ground.

"Feeble minded vagabonds," Kayla said to Titus. She pointed at Charlie. "This one is mute, and the other talks nonsense."

Her superior attitude was getting to me. "You don't know everything," I said.

She pushed me forward. "And you do? We'll see how smart you are when Lucius arrives."

The driveway led to the front of the house, where a grand, double-door entry was, but we didn't go that way. We took a path around to the back, where it wasn't so grand. It was still big, and impressive, but the pavement gave way to hard-packed earth and the large yard contained several outbuildings and a dozen or so wagons in a variety of sizes and styles. Weeds grew around disorganized piles of wood and bricks, and a collection of what looked like old-fashioned farming equipment in various states of repair, were laid up against a stone wall.

"Mother will know where we can find Lucius," Kayla said. "I will go ask her."

Titus poked Charlie in the back with his saw. "I'll have that garment now, boy."

To my surprise, Charlie let the cloak slip to the ground. As Titus bent to take it, Charlie continued to stare at his feet, his shoulders slumped, looking submissive and beaten. And that's when I knew there'd be trouble.

"No, Charlie!"

But he'd already spun and hit Titus in the head, stunning him. Then he grabbed Titus's saw and, using it like we had been taught to use the staffs, he gave Cassius, who ran up to help Titus, a one-two hit— shoulder, kidney—that left him sprawled in the dirt. His medieval weapons instructor would have been pleased.

I ran toward him as Titus got to his feet and Kayla rushed him. He raised the saw to strike her.

"Stop."

I lunged at him, getting in front of Kayla, grabbing his arm.

"Let me go," he said.

"This isn't helping. You're going to make things worse."

I waited for Kayla to hit me or wrap her hands around my throat. But that didn't happen. And Titus, now on his feet, hadn't come for us, either. Even Cassius, lying on his back and propped up by his elbows merely stared at us. Then another voice came, calm but commanding. "Hold. Lay aside your weapon."

I looked and saw a woman—tall and thin, with red hair and eyes like Kayla's—coming our way. I let go of Charlie and he slowly lowered the saw. The woman marched toward us, but when I stepped away from Charlie she stopped. The colour drained from her face, and she raised a hand to her cheek.

The yard went silent. The woman gazed at us with a mixture of fear and wonder.

"It's you," she said.

Chapter 6

"His markings," Cassius said. "Surely this is powerful sorcery."

He was staring at Charlie's pyjama top, with the picture of Luke Skywalker swinging his light sabre. It made sense; they'd never seen a photo-transfer on a tee-shirt before, or a photo, or a tee-shirt for that matter. Given that context, it could easily be mistaken for magic.

Titus, who was behind Charlie, took a step back. Hearing the noise, Charlie turned and raised the saw again, causing Titus to retreat further and giving the others a look at his back, where Darth Vader wielded his own light sabre.

Cassius gasped and scrambled—crab-like, on his elbows and feet—to where the woman stood, still holding a hand to the side of her whitened face. Only Kayla looked as if she still had any fight in her, but even she stared and made no move toward us.

"He has the markings of the two-faced goddess," Titus said. "They have been sent by the gods."

This was our chance, and I was trying to think of a way to work it to our advantage when the woman spoke.

"It is the prophecy," she said, her voice heavy. "Two boys. A warrior and a peacemaker. Wanderers, carrying a cloak." Then she looked straight at me. "You are brothers. This is true, is it not?"

I nodded, now as mesmerized as the others. I bent and picked up the cloak, still lying at Charlie's feet.

"Mother, no," Kayla said. She made no move toward us or away from us, or toward her mother, but she kept her eyes steadily fixed on mine. "They lie."

But the woman ignored her and came closer.

"You have come to return what was taken. To restore our people. To save the Land."

I had no answer for this, and then another voice came from behind.

"They have come to make me a rich man."

"Lucius," the woman said, pointing at us, "the prophecy—"

A broad-shouldered man wearing a mud-spattered tunic strode into view. He stood very close, between us and the woman, with his fists on his hips.

"These are the two who've been sneaking around on my farm?"

"We weren't sneaking," Charlie said. I saw, with no small relief, that he didn't challenge the man with the saw, and instead dropped it on the ground.

"This is true," I said. "Please let us go."

"Release thieves?" Lucius laughed. "So you can report to your masters, and lead raiders back to steal more?"

"We're not raiders," Charlie and I said in unison.

"They were caught in my house," Kayla said, "looking for valuables."

The woman stepped up next to him. "Lucius, the prophecy."

"You cling like a weening babe to your gods," Lucius said. "These boys are nothing but common thieves. They are too valuable to let go."

The colour returned to the woman's face, only now it was red. Kayla, too, looked at Lucius with an expression of concern.

"Husband," the woman said, "you take a dangerous path."

"There is no gain without danger. To release these boys would be an insult to the gods."

"But our life here is good. You look to your gods for gain instead of thanking them for what you have."

Lucius waved a hand at us. "And here is the answer from the gods."

When I realized Lucius was only after money, I thought to offer him ours, but before I could, he ordered Cassius to his feet.

"Lock them in the bathhouse."

Both Cassius and Titus hesitated.

"The magic …"

Lucius stepped forward and pulled Charlie's tee-shirt roughly over his head.

"Hey!"

Back in Wynantskill, Charlie would have been considered tanned and big for his age, but compared to the others, he looked puny and pale.

"There is no magic here," Lucius said, throwing the tee-shirt to his wife. "They are mere flesh and blood. Take them." He turned to his wife. "And bring them proper clothing."

Titus picked up his saw, but he didn't try to prod Charlie with it.

"Did you encounter anyone on your way here?" Lucius demanded.

"No one," Cassius said. "Several saw us, but we exchanged no words."

Lucius rubbed a hand over the stubble on his chin.

"Then these boys were not the raiders. You brought them here, and I released them." He looked to Cassius and Titus. "You understand?"

They both nodded.

"Any word," Lucius said, "even a whisper, that these boys have not moved on, and you will find yourselves in the mines. Now swear to me."

"Lucius," the woman said, "this path leads only to sorrow."

"Silence, woman," Lucius said, still looking at Cassius and Titus. "Now swear."

Both Cassius and Titus bobbed their heads.

"I swear," Titus said.

"And I," Cassius added.

Lucius nodded, looking pleased. "Good. Now take them to the bathhouse. Lock them in. Make certain it is secure."

Cassius took me by an arm. Lucius grabbed the cloak and pulled it from my hands.

"Hey, that's ours."

Lucius held the cloak up, admiring it. "You surely are thieves. No one such as you would own a garment as fine as this."

"It was a gift from our grandfather," I said. "It belongs to us."

Lucius nodded. "I would believe that is so, for it means this cloak is surely mine."

"You can't just take our stuff," Charlie said.

Lucius began folding the cloak. "You have no possessions," he said, turning away and walking toward the villa. "What was yours is now mine."

"You can't pull that on us," Charlie called after him. "We're not your pages."

Lucius stopped but didn't turn to face us. "I know

nothing of pages," he said. "You are my slaves." He looked over his shoulder at Cassius and Titus. "Now lock them away."

Chapter 7

"Slaves," Charlie said. "What does he mean by that?"

The bathhouse didn't have a bathtub in it. Whatever it used to be, it was now used for storing hay. It was made of rough stones and was at least twenty feet tall. There were a few horizontal slits high up by the beamed ceiling that let in light, but otherwise, it was dark and gloomy and smelled of damp. The oak door, which had slammed solidly behind us, didn't budge when we tried to push it open, so we sat down next to it and stared into the gloom.

"I guess it's sorta like being a page boy, only more permanent."

"But he can't do that."

I wished he was right, but the little I knew about ancient Rome assured me that he wasn't. Rome was a slave culture, and it looked like we had been taken as slaves. And who was there to stop him? The only thing I was glad about was that I hadn't given him the money. Both bags were still in my pockets because they hadn't thought to search me, and now I was afraid it might occur to them. And even if it didn't, they were going to bring us different clothes and, presumably, take ours. I didn't want the money to still be with me when that happened.

"We've got to hide these," I said, pulling the leather

bags out of my pockets.

"What for? You heard him. Our stuff is his now."

"But he doesn't know we have this. If we can keep it, we might be able to use it."

"So, hide them, then," he said, standing and walking away from me. "Just leave me out of it." He wrapped his arms around himself and kicked at the ground, sending up clouds of hay. "I'm cold and tired and I want to go home."

"So do I," I said, "and this might help us. Now look for a place to hide it."

The walls were sturdy and well-built, with no spaces between the stones, and the ground was too hard to dig in, especially without any tools.

"Maybe over there," Charlie said, pushing his way through the pile of hay to get to the far wall. Then he dropped out of sight.

"Charlie!"

"I think I found the bathtub."

I went to help him and sank over my head as the floor disappeared. We had to practically swim through the hay to get back to where we had been standing.

"That's too big to be a bathtub," Charlie said.

"I think it's a sort of shallow swimming pool. That's what the Romans would call a bathhouse."

"They must have needed storage more than they needed a bath."

"Whatever," I said, "but it's a good place to hide the money."

"What? You'll never find it again, assuming you can get back in here, that is."

"Unless you a have a better idea."

I felt my way along the edge of the pool, using my foot. When I found the corner, I lowered myself into the hay. "Help me dig, Charlie."

Reluctantly, Charlie came into the pool with me. It was about four feet deep, and we had to dig into the matted hay to find the bottom corner. Dust swirled about us, making it hard to breathe, but we dug deeper and soon found where the walls met a smooth, stone floor.

"If we put the bags here, they should stay, and we should be able to find them again."

I nestled them into the corner. The hay squeaked and something fat and furry brushed against my arm before scurrying away.

"There are things in here besides us," Charlie said.

I pressed the bags into the corner and piled hay on them.

"That's good enough. Let's get out of here."

Back on the ground, we brushed hay out of our hair and off our clothes. Charlie's arms and back were scratched and blotched with red but there was nothing we could do about that. A minute later, the latch clanked, and the door opened, blinding us with sunlight.

The silhouette that appeared in the doorway turned out to be the woman, Kayla's mother, with a bundle cradled in one arm. She closed the door but didn't latch it. We could have made a break for it, but there was the cloak, and the money.

"Sit," she said, "we have much to talk about."

She sat cross-legged on the floor, and we sat in front of her, making a small triangle with her at the point. She placed the bundle in front of us.

"These are new clothes for you. You must wear them. Your garments mark you as strangers, and people are wary of the unknown."

42

We picked through the bundle. There were two long, loose shirts, low shoes with wooden soles and soft leather sides, and a length of cloth I was pretty sure was supposed to take the place of our underwear.

Charlie and I looked at each other but neither of us made a move.

"Your modesty is misplaced," the woman said, "but I will turn if you prefer, and speak while you change."

When her back was to us, we undressed and pulled on the shirts and pants. By unspoken agreement, we kept our own underwear and slipped the Roman underwear under the hay behind us where she couldn't see it. The shirts were of a course material—not as fine or brilliant white like the gown the woman was wearing—and had strings of leather for belts. When we put them on, they looked like knee-length skirts, which would normally have had us in hysterics, but neither of us even smiled. As we dressed the woman spoke in a steady voice that seemed to fill the room.

"My name is Ameena, wife of Cyril, a Celtic warrior, and daughter of a Celtic chief. I lived in the plains, free and at one with the Land. Then, when I was still a girl, no older than Kayla, a prophecy was bestowed upon me.

"I was a rebellious child, refusing to believe the elders' teachings. But my father believed the gods had a purpose for me. He brought me to the stone circle and bid me look into the sacred mirror as the first rays of the summer solstice shone over the horizon. And in that stone, I saw a vision."

By this time, we had finished dressing, but we sat quietly behind her, taking in her voice, not wanting to disturb her, for she seemed in a trance as she spoke.

"The stone drew me in. What I saw terrified me. All

43

around was blood, and pain and loss. I saw my world set on fire and ripped from my hands. And when I thought my heart could take no more, I saw two boys, brothers—twins, yet not twins—who had travelled from far away, carrying a cloak. And a voice told me they were the ones who would return what was taken, who would restore my people, and save the Land. Those boys were you."

Her words felt heavy. If she had been waiting for us all this time to fix things up, she should be glad to see us. But she seemed terribly sad.

"I'm sure whatever you saw, whoever you saw, it wasn't us."

She shook her head slowly. It wasn't the reaction I was expecting. She obviously, sincerely believed in what she was saying, and people with deep convictions were often emotional, so I was surprised she didn't protest, or raise her voice.

"You are the ones," she said, her voice low. "Brothers. Summer twins, born after the same solstice, of Celtic blood. You know this to be true."

"Okay, we have red hair," Charlie said. "But so do a lot of people."

"We really don't know what you're talking about," I said, "and even if we did, I'm pretty sure we can't help you. We can't even help ourselves."

She turned around, settled herself and looked from me to Charlie. "You understand more than you realize. You belong to these events, and you will play your part, just as I must. My husband, Lucius, is a good man, but his desire for riches will be his downfall. He seeks to thwart the prophecy, but it will not be denied. Tragedy awaits."

"If you're so certain we're part of your prophecy,"

Charlie said, "can't you let us go?"

Ameena bowed her head. "Would that I could. The gods are turning the wheels now, and we are moving to their will." She looked toward the unlocked door. "You are free to run, if you desire, but you cannot outrun the gods, and I cannot roll time back, no matter how my heart wishes I could."

I got the idea that part of her wanted us to run, even though she knew it wouldn't do any good. Then the pieces of her rambling monologue came together for me, and I sensed where her sorrow was coming from.

"You said your husband's name was Cyril, but your husband is Lucius."

Ameena nodded. "Yes. In the years following my vision, I married a warrior. Cyril was a brave man, as brave as my father. And when the Romans attacked our settlement, they fought them. One of the Roman commanders killed my husband, and my father, and took Kayla and I as slaves. That Roman was Fabianus, the master of this farm. It is he who ripped the sacred stone from my village, from the heart of my people. And it is you who will get it back."

"Much as we'd love to do that," Charlie said, "we don't know anything about any Fabianus, or a sacred stone, or how to get out of here, even."

"But you know of the goddess who imbues the stone with power," Ameena said, her voice suddenly stronger. "You wore her markings: a noble warrior and a warrior with a black heart. One good, one evil, two sides to reflect her two faces, and the two sides of the stone."

I felt a sudden bloom of ice in my chest. "You're talking about the Talisman," I said.

Charlie's mouth dropped slowly open. "No. Oh,

45

no," he said. "You looked into it, didn't you, with a stalwart heart?"

Ameena's shoulders sagged. She nodded slowly. "Yes. And it showed me the truth. And the truth is, you are the ones."

She stood, gathered our discarded clothes, and went to the door. I watched her go, the feeling of cold terror still with me. Her long-awaited prophecy had arrived, yet Ameena looked anything but relieved. What else had she seen?

"Why are you sad?" I asked as she opened the door. "If our destiny is to save the Land and return the Talisman, why are you not happy."

"Because," she said, stepping into the sunshine, "in doing so, you will take my daughter from me."

Chapter 8

"Maybe she's not talking about Kayla," Charlie said. "Maybe she's got another daughter."

We were sitting with our backs against the wall, listening to our stomachs growl, and waiting, because there was nothing else to do. We'd arrived in the morning and had been locked in the bathhouse about an hour and a half later. I estimated about two hours had passed since then, which made it lunch time. And that explained why we were both hungry.

"You know that's not the case," I said. "But that does give us some hope."

Charlie said nothing; he just looked at me with disbelief.

"Seriously," I said, "if we do manage to escape, there is no way that girl would want to come with us, and no way we could force her to. And that's assuming we'd want her with us, which we don't. So, if that part of Ameena's prophecy is wrong, maybe she's wrong about all of it."

Charlie settled back against the wall. "I don't know whether that's an optimistic outlook, or if you're simply deluded."

I said nothing. The answer was obvious.

A few minutes later the door latch clanked, and daylight cut the darkness.

"Come," a voice said.

We went to the door and found Lucius and Titus there, standing next to a horse and cart. The cart was made of rough boards and had a bundle of what looked like burlap in it. At first glance, I thought Titus still had his saw, but a second glance revealed it to be an actual spear, and he had a knife in his belt, as did Lucius.

"Into the cart with you," Lucius said. "And cover yourselves."

A dozen questions came to mind, but Lucius didn't look in the mood to answer them, so I climbed into the cart, and Charlie came after me. We pulled the bulky blanket, which was more like a tarp, over us and sat, once again, in darkness. Then a corner of the tarp lifted, and Lucius tossed a small bundle at us.

"Eat now," he said. "And give no thought to escaping. Titus will ride in the cart with you. If you move, he will kill you."

Darkness returned. The cart wobbled and creaked as Titus and Lucius climbed aboard, then we nearly fell over as the cart lurched forward. We bounced against the boards, and I had to clench my jaw to keep my teeth from rattling together. Dust rose between the cracks, making us sneeze, and bringing with it the smell of horse.

The cart clip-clopped out of the farmyard, but we weren't heading for the road. Instead, we went the other way, along a road we hadn't been on before. I tried to keep track of where we were heading but almost immediately lost my sense of direction, so we concentrated on trying to eat the bread and cheese Lucius had given us, while being bounced around like loose luggage. There was also a skin of water, which went down a lot easier.

The cart turned left, then left, then right, and after

that I lost count. About fifteen minutes later, we came to a stop and the tarp was flung off us. "Out now," Lucius said, "time for work."

We were in another field, a large one, bordered by low trees. Leafy plants grew in neat rows over much of it.

"A mild winter and a hot spring blessed us with an early turnip crop," Lucius said as we got down from the cart. "It needs harvesting."

"We're not farmers," Charlie said.

"You are whatever I say you are," Lucius said, unhitching the horse from the cart. "Titus, remember what I told you."

"Yes, Lucius," Titus said, nodding.

"If you let them escape, I'll see you branded."

Titus grabbed my arm. "They will go nowhere."

I think he meant to give me a shake, but he stopped and looked at me with a puzzled expression and a furrowed brow.

"Lucius," he said. "There is no strength in him." He ran his hand down my arm, massaging my muscles, then felt my fingers. "And his hands are soft. They speak true. They are not accustomed to field work."

"Then they must have been house slaves," Lucius said.

"We're not slaves," Charlie said.

Lucius took the horse by the reins. "So you say."

"We do," I said. "You can't believe we're slaves. If we are, then you're holding stolen property. And you know we're not robbers. You may be a slave society, but you can't pluck free people off the street and make slaves of them."

Lucius led the horse away, turning to go back the way we had come.

"If he speaks again," Lucius said without looking back, "beat him. But do not mark his face."

The three of us watched Lucius and the horse until they disappeared around the trees.

"We work now," Titus said. But he didn't try to touch me.

"He's taken us illegally," I said. It wasn't a question.

"If he's breaking the law by having us," Charlie said, "then we can just go." He looked at Titus, and his spear. "You're not really going to kill us, are you?"

Titus, instead of asserting his authority, looked terrified.

"Please," he said, "if I allow you to escape, Lucius will have me branded. I have been nothing but loyal since my capture, and if I am branded, I can never be a citizen."

Charlie started shuffling away. "So? That's your look out. You're the one that got us into this mess. We were just lost, and you turned us in to Lucius."

Titus turned toward Charlie and sank to his knees. "I didn't know. You were in Kayla's house. I thought you were thieves. I didn't realize. Not until …"

I suddenly understood that we had the advantage. "Yes," I said. "You saw his markings. You heard Ameena's prophecy. You know we shouldn't have been taken as slaves. So let us go."

Titus shook his head, clearly distraught. "I can't. I am duty bound. If one of you runs, I am to cut a foot off the one who didn't. If you both run, I am to cut off the foot of the first one who is caught. And you will be caught, because there is no place to run to. I swore an oath; I cannot break it."

I looked at Charlie and motioned for him to come back. I was pleased that he did, seeing as how I was the one about to lose a foot.

"We don't want him branded, Charlie," I said, "and he's right—we'd be caught in a heartbeat."

"I am sorry," Titus said, and I believed he meant it. "If it were up to me, I would let you go. But two handsome boys, sold in the Londinium marketplace, would fetch enough to fill an emperor's purse, and this is too much for Lucius to pass up."

Charlie looked crestfallen. "So, if we're not going to escape, what are we going to do?"

"I don't know," I said, "But if Lucius is after money, he has other, safer, ways of getting it."

Charlie nodded at me. "And you have a plan?"

"No," I said, "but I'm working on one."

Titus got to his feet, still holding the spear but without much conviction. "We must work now," he said. "Titus will want this cart full by the time he returns, and the day is half spent."

The work was picking turnips, which wasn't as easy as it should have been. The ground was baked hard, making it difficult to pull them out, then the leaves had to be separated from the root and Titus had to do that because he was the one with the knife. And once that was done, we had to carry them to the cart. It was a lot of wasted effort, and after half an hour went by with little accomplished—aside from us getting sweaty and filthy—Titus began to look worried.

"We will not have the cart half-filled at this rate," he said, slicing the greens from another turnip and putting the two parts in separate baskets. "We need to work faster."

"No," I said, "we need to work smarter."

I thought he might get angry that I had challenged him, but he merely looked puzzled. "What are you

51

saying?"

Charlie sat down and wiped his brow, looking relieved for the break. Titus remained squatting between the two baskets, holding his machete-like knife. Both of them looked at me, waiting.

"Charlie is better at pulling the turnips up, and you," I said, pointing at Titus, "have the knife, so you need to cut them. I can go behind you, gathering the turnips and the leaves into the baskets and taking them to the cart. That way, we can just keep moving down a row and have it done in no time."

I saw Charlie scowling at me and realized he wasn't happy with my plan.

"And on the next row," I added hastily, "I can pull up the turnips and Charlie can carry the baskets."

This seemed to satisfy everyone, and after Titus showed how we were to deposit the harvest in the cart—turnips in the wagon, greens on the tarp lying on the ground—we set to work. The assembly-line took some effort to get moving, but once it got in motion, we finished the row in record time. Then we finished another, and another. And then the cart was full.

"We don't want to harvest any more," Titus said, "or the turnips will bounce out on our return journey."

We arranged the load in the cart to be as stable as possible, then bundled the tarp—filled with the greens—and arranged it on top. Then we waited.

Titus got a skin of water and passed it around. "Lucius will not have expected us to finish so soon," he said, sitting in what little shade the cart provided. "When he comes, make like we have just finished, or tomorrow he will make us fill a larger cart."

That made sense to me. I sat in the shade with him, wiped the sweat from my forehead, massaged my sore

52

hands and arms and took a long drink from the skin.

"You are not accustomed to hard work," Titus observed.

"No, we're not," I said, looking at Charlie, who was lying in the dirt, his hands folded over his chest, already half asleep. "And we're certainly not used to being slaves."

"You have slaves to do this work for you?"

I shook my head. "No. We have no slaves at all. In our land, slavery does not exist."

It took a while for Titus to respond. His expression went from shock, to bewilderment, to disbelief, to amusement. "Surely you are joking."

"Not at all," I said. "We used to have slavery, but it was outlawed long ago."

"Because it's wrong," Charlie said, without opening his eyes.

"What land is this? Where did you travel from?"

I didn't know enough about ancient Rome to come up with a reasonable lie, so I told him the truth.

"Wynatskill," I said. I didn't add that it was about two-thousand years in the future.

Titus sighed and looked at the cloudless sky. "It sounds a marvellous land. I should like to go."

"It's far away," I said.

Titus looked disappointed. "But when I am free, I could travel there? Yes?"

Now it was my turn to look bewildered. "When you're free? But you're a slave."

"I was not born a slave," he said, with some amount of indignation. "I was taken. And soon I will be liberti."

"Lib what?" Charlie asked, his eyes still shut.

"Liberti," Titus said, "a former slave. That's what I will become after I buy my freedom."

This caused my heart to pound so hard against my ribs that I thought he might hear it. Charlie sat up. "Hey, we could—"

I cut him off with a warning look.

"You can buy your freedom?" I asked, trying to sound casual.

"Of course," he said. "My wife is liberti. We bought her freedom three years ago. We live in the village. She launders garments and does needlework for money. We will soon have enough to buy my freedom."

I struggled to keep a straight face. It was a lot of information to take in.

"You don't live on the farm, in slave quarters?"

Titus shrugged. "I used to. But when we bought my wife's freedom, we moved into the village."

"And now you, what?" Charlie asked. "Get up in the morning and report to Lucius, like it's a job?"

Titus looked puzzled again. "I'm a slave," he said, as if that answered the question.

"But you won't always be," I said, "because you can buy your freedom."

"How much does it cost?" Charlie asked, before Titus could answer.

"It's not as easy as that," he said. "I know it must confuse you, never having been a slave, and never having owned one."

"Then how much did you pay Lucius for your wife's freedom," Charlie asked. "And how much are you going to pay him for yours?"

Titus looked puzzled again. "Lucius? I don't pay Lucius. I pay Fabianus. It is he who owns us all." Then he laughed. "And what good fortune that is. Fabianus has much wealth and Lucius has little. That makes Lucius drive a harder bargain."

"But Lucius runs this farm," Charlie said. "And he lives in that big house. He's not exactly poor."

Titus nodded. "He has a good life, but no wealth. He may own this farm one day, for he has let it be known that Fabianus favours him and will give him the farm when he grants him his freedom, but many believe that to be a dream."

My head spun. "His freedom? Lucius is a slave?"

Titus nodded. "Of course."

"But … but," Charlie said, "he can't have us as slaves then, if he's a slave himself."

Titus ran a hand over his face. "You ask too many questions. Of course, he can have slaves. You are vicarii, a slave of a slave."

"But …" A myriad of questions formed, all vying to be asked first, and I found I couldn't form a sentence. Before I could sort them out Titus's gaze shifted from me to something in the distance.

"Quiet," he said, his eyes suddenly alert. "He comes. Up, quickly, and look industrious."

Chapter 9

The turnip storage shed was one of the out-buildings near the villa, where our bathhouse-prison was. Lucius had made me and Charlie lie flat against the sides of the wagon, on top of the turnips, on the ride back. The turnips softened the bumps, and I got to look at a little scenery, so the ride back wasn't as bad as the ride out, and it strengthened my conviction that Lucius—despite Titus's assertions—was doing something he shouldn't.

He was happy lording it over us, and making sure we knew we were his slaves, but he was keeping us out of sight. We had been the only three harvesting that field, whereas there were dozens working the fields and orchards we passed on the way back. And the farmyard, as we added the turnips to the mound in the storage shed, remained strangely deserted.

"We did well today," Titus said, sucking up to Lucius while Charlie and I dumped another basket of turnips on the growing pile.

Lucius stood with his fists on his hips—his favourite pose—looking doubtful.

"Sometimes, too much of a good thing can turn into a bad thing," he said, staring at the growing mountain. "I fear this is not to our advantage."

"But Lucius," Titus said, waving a hand at Turnip Mountain, "all this bounty."

They were pointedly ignoring us, treating us like we weren't there, like we were slaves.

"It's about supply and demand," I said as I walked past them with another basket-load. "A surplus supply and low demand make the price go down. If it gets bad enough, you'll end up selling them at a loss. The only thing you can do then is hold on to them until the demand rises. We learned that in school."

Lucius's face went red, and I thought I'd better stop before I went too far, but Charlie picked it up, adding his own take.

"If you have stuff you can't sell, you need to create a market for it. You could do candied turnips on a stick, or sell pet turnips, something like that."

That pushed him over the edge. He grabbed us both by an arm, making us spill turnips everywhere.

"Silence. Back to your quarters."

He marched us toward the bathhouse, making me struggle to stay on my feet.

"Our grandfather," I said, puffing as he dragged us along, "he's a wealthy man. And generous. I could contact him. He would pay you. Then you will have money, and you can let us go."

"Silence," was all he said.

"You're taking a risk," I continued. "Someone is bound to see us. Someone will talk. You'll be found out. Let us go and we will make you wealthy."

It seemed to have no impact. Without a word, he shoved us into the bathhouse, slammed the door and threw the bolt.

"That could have gone better," Charlie said.

I kicked some hay into a pile near the wall and sat on it.

"Yes, it could have," I said, "but he's got something

to think about now. That stuff I said about supply and demand, it wasn't just to taunt him. It was the truth, and something he's worried about. And now he's been shown a way he can get out of this and make a profit."

"Yeah," Charlie said, slumping down beside me. "By taking our money, and then selling us as slaves to the highest bidder."

I stared into the gloom, watching the hay and the far walls slowly appear as my eyes adjusted to the dark. My face glowed from the sun, my arms and hands ached, and an empty pit in my stomach grew larger and colder. Charlie was probably right, but there was no sense dwelling on that.

I must have dozed, because I was jolted awake by the clanking of the latch. Then I felt a stabbing pain in my eyes as daylight flooded in. A wooden bucket, with water sloshing over the edges, thumped down in front of us.

"For washing," Lucius said, "not drinking. Food will be brought shortly."

Then he walked away.

"What about a bathroom break?" Charlie called after him. "Or do you want me to piss all over your hay?"

Lucius stopped and turned to face us. "Are you blind? There is a privy there." He pointed toward the back wall. "Or are you so poor you shit in a hole in the ground? Rich grandfather, indeed." Then he left, slamming the door behind him.

We went to the back wall, careful to skirt around the pool, and found a strange-looking seat made of stone.

"This must be it," Charlie said. "Doesn't look like it has been used in a while, which is good. Can you imagine the smell?"

I could.

Thirsty as we were, the water didn't tempt us. It was obviously run off from a bathtub or something. But it was good enough to wash in. We used our discarded Roman underwear—one as a washcloth and the other as a towel—and felt miles better for it. Shortly after we finished, the door opened again. This time, Kayla came in. I looked past her, through the door, and noticed— in the slice of light I could see—that the shadows in the yard were getting long. Evening was coming.

"If I had known they were going to make me your slave," she said, setting a tray of food in front of us, "I would have killed you when I had the chance."

She carried our washing bucket into the yard and came back with a bloated skin that I hoped contained water. It didn't. When she dropped it at our feet, I greedily sucked on it and immediately gagged. Charlie grabbed it and, ignoring my reaction, drank and sputtered.

"Are you trying to poison us?"

The liquid tasted sour, leaving my throat dry and my mouth puckered. I picked up some bread and bit off a hunk. It didn't help.

"It's the same wine we drink," Kayla said. "Or it might be what we give to the field workers. I can't recall."

She sat, cross-legged, in front of us. Her knee-length dress—made from a fine, white fabric and arranged in symmetrical folds—rode up to her thighs as she sat, revealing white skin. She may have been a slave, but she had an easier life than Titus. Her red hair was down now, falling around her shoulders. On her feet were sandals, laced up her calves with crisscrossed strips of leather. She glared at us and pulled her dress down to cover her knees. "Eat."

She had left the door open. The light was welcome, but also tempting. Both Charlie and I looked longingly at it.

Kayla smiled. "Go ahead. Run," she said. Then she produced a knife. A small one, but with a thin, lethal-looking blade. "I look forward to it."

We ate in silence for a while, occasionally sipping at the sour liquid in the skin. I began to wonder why Ameena, with her fears about us taking Kayla away from her, had allowed her to bring us food.

"Why you?" I asked between mouthfuls.

Kayla's brow furrowed. "What do you mean?"

"Why are you bringing us food? You are not, as you point out, our slave."

"You don't ask," she said. "You are told."

"It's just that, your mother seems afraid we're going to take you away from her. I'd think she wouldn't want you anywhere near us."

"My mother's prophetic vision is a fantasy from her youth," Kayla said. Then she held up the dagger again. "And I can take care of myself."

This was a revelation.

"If you don't believe in the prophecy," I said, "then why are you so afraid of us?"

"Afraid? I fear nothing, least of all you two."

I kept eating. The bread was soft, the meat tender, and there was cheese, and some cut up fruit. It would have been nice with some lemonade, or drinkable water. All the while, Kayla watched us, her eyes wary, her thumb fingering the blade of her knife.

"You've mentioned several times," I said, trying another sip of the wine, noting that, this time, it didn't taste as bad, "that you want to kill us. People mostly kill out of hate, or fear. You don't know us well enough to hate us, so you must be afraid."

"I told you," Kayla said. "I fear nothing."

I shrugged. "So, you hate us. But hate also springs from fear."

Kayla pulled the tray away, even though we had not finished eating. "You speak too much."

"I speak true," I said.

Kayla rose, taking the tray with her.

"We're a threat to you," I said as she walked toward the door. "What Lucius is doing. If he's found out, you stand to lose everything: your fine clothes, your good food, your soft bed."

She stepped through the door, not looking back.

"Unless you let us go, all that will be taken from you."

The only reply was the slamming of the door.

"Your skin will no longer be white and soft," I shouted. "It will be baked to leather by the sun."

Darkness returned, and silence.

◆

"What the hell is wrong with you?"

It wasn't the first time Charlie had asked me that. It was full dark now. The light had long since stopped glowing in the slits high in the walls. Charlie took another sip from the wineskin and passed it to me. "What do you think you're going to accomplish by making everyone mad at us?"

I squeezed the last of the wine into my mouth. It still tasted sour, but I didn't care.

"I wanted to make them see the error of their ways."

Even I had to laugh at that.

"Good job," Charlie said, snickering. "And what was all that about her soft, white thighs?"

"I never mentioned her thighs. I didn't."

"But that's what you were thinking of."

I tried to wring more wine out of the empty skin and failed.

"Yeah, I guess I was."

Charlie picked up the flaccid wineskin, inspected it and tossed it away. "What do we do now?"

"Sleep," I said.

And for some reason, even that caused us to laugh.

We gathered up two piles of hay and, using the Roman underwear for pillows (I took the damp one since it was my fault we had to go to bed without our full dinner), settled down for the night, spiralling into slumber, despite the cloying scent of hay and the sound of burrowing rats.

Chapter 10

A thud, followed by a toe nudging me in the side, woke me. I opened my eyes with some difficulty, as they were welded shut with grit. My mouth was dry and tasted sour, and a dull ache throbbed behind my forehead. The thud had been a pile of blankets dropped between me and Charlie, and the toe that nudged me belonged to Lucius. He didn't look happy. I sat up, and the room spun.

"Eat," Lucius said, "and be ready in ten minutes."

"Ready for what?" Charlie asked, rubbing his eyes.

Lucius grunted and headed for the door. "Work."

"We did that yesterday," Charlie said. "Can't we do something else today?"

Lucius ignored him. "And no talking. You have unsettled my wife, upset her daughter, and even Titus is reluctant to work with you."

"Maybe you should let us go, then," I said.

Lucius had his back to us, but I saw him stiffen. He seemed under a lot of stress, and I thought maybe I should stop pushing him. He halted at the doorway.

"You will work with Titus. You will not talk." Then he sighed. "I fear my wife's prophecy is coming true—you are becoming more trouble than you are worth." He looked over his shoulder at us. "So, if you run, if you make a nuisance of yourselves, I will gladly have you killed."

He stepped outside. The door slammed shut.

"Way to go, Mitch," Charlie said, groping for the food Lucius had left behind.

"Me? Why is it my fault?"

"All your 'making them see the error of their ways.'"

I grabbed some of the food and took a drink from the skin that contained—I was please to discover—water. "Well, it's having an effect."

"I don't call Lucius wanting to kill us progress."

I ate in silence. He had a point.

"Well, at least we have blankets now."

True to his word, Lucius was back before we had even finished eating. He ordered us outside, where Titus and, as predicted, a larger cart waited. We laid down in the back and Lucius drove, with Titus sitting, unarmed, beside him.

We bounced about in the wagon bed as Lucius urged the horse on. We travelled fast and I wondered if it was because Lucius didn't want to be seen, or if he was enjoying our discomfort, or a combination of the two.

We travelled to the same field we had been in the previous day, and like the previous day, Lucius unhitched the horse and led it away, but not before giving us one final warning.

"You will not be guarded as you were yesterday, because Titus has assured me you will not run. Therefore, if you do, I will have to kill him, as well as you."

With that, he and the horse left the field and walked back up the lane.

"He's in a good mood this morning," Charlie said.

"You are not to talk," Titus said. "You asked too many questions yesterday."

"I'm not asking a question," Charlie said. "I'm making an observation. Lucius is in a foul mood."

Titus nodded. "He is. We have word that Fabianus is in Londinium. He may stop here on his way back to his villa by the sea. That will be bad for Lucius."

"Because he is not supposed to have us as slaves," I said.

Titus groaned and shook his head, pressing his hands to his temples. "There are other considerations," he said, "but what you say is true. Fabianus will be most displeased if he finds you. It will not go well for Lucius, or any of us. I fear bad things are coming, very bad things."

I looked at Charlie and smiled. We may have been forbidden to talk to Titus, but Lucius wasn't going to be able to make Titus stop talking to us.

The day was as warm and sunny as the previous one, but at least this time we were given straw hats to protect us, and we had an ample amount of drinking water and food. We went back to our assembly line method and, by lunch time, had the wagon filled with turnips and their greens. We rested, ate, drank, and an hour later, Lucius returned to find us working hard and the wagon nearly full.

He didn't seem to be in as dark a mood. The tension was gone from his face, and he wasn't sharp with Titus over some perceived lack of diligence. He didn't even complain about having more useless turnips to store and try to sell at the local markets. And, after we returned to the farm and unloaded, instead of sending us back out with another cart—even though there was plenty of daylight left—he locked us in the bathhouse, with water and food, and left us alone.

"Maybe he took on board my suggestion that we do

something different today," Charlie said, biting into a hunk of cheese.

I sat down next to him but didn't touch the food. "No, something's changed. I don't like this."

Charlie looked up at the ceiling, shaking his head. "What is it with you? You annoy him until he wants to kill us, and that's fine, but now that he's treating us better, you think something's wrong."

I picked up some bread and sliced meat and made a makeshift sandwich. "It just seems strange, that's all. We need to be cautious."

The afternoon dragged on. Charlie observed that it would go quicker if we had a television and a Play Station. I agreed with him, but thought some books would suit me better, preferably books on Roman history. I mentally kicked myself for not having read any before we went on this adventure. I'd read a lot of history, but very little on Rome, and anything I did read had concentrated on the city of Rome and things like the Colosseum. I wasn't even aware that they had conquered England.

The hours ticked by. The patches of sunlight filtering in through the high, narrow windows, moved across the walls, and grew dim. Then the door opened, and Kayla entered.

"I have laid a meal for you," she said, standing near the opening. "You may come outside to eat, but you have to promise not to run."

"Yes, of course," Charlie said, "or you'll kill us."

She smiled. "No. But you will be caught."

Charlie nodded. "And someone else will kill us."

"Almost certainly. Now come."

We stepped out the door. Not far away, she—or other servants—had set up a small table with three stools. On the table was a feast. Chicken, cooked vegetables, bread, cheese, wine glasses, plates. It looked almost modern.

We sat, and Kayla sat across from us.

"Now eat," she said. "I will be your hostess."

She poured wine from a clay jug into our tin cups, and then poured some for herself, into a silver goblet. When we both just stared at her in disbelief, she waved a pale hand at us. "Go ahead, eat. Don't mind me."

Cautiously, I took a bite. It didn't seem poisoned.

Charlie ate some and took a drink of wine. "This is good," he said slowly. "Thank you, Kayla." Then he turned to me. "I think you were right." He smiled as he said it, but his eyes flicked Kayla's way.

Kayla sipped her wine. She had on the same type of clothing as the previous day, but her hair was now piled on top of her head, with delicate ringlets cascading down each side of her face. Behind her, I saw the sun, slowly easing toward the distant horizon, its rays making her gown and hair glow. She looked like an angel, but one I remained wary of.

"Not talking?" she asked, taking another drink from her goblet.

"We're not supposed to talk to you," Charlie said. "Lucius says we upset you."

Kayla shrugged. "It will be a boring dinner party if you won't talk. So, I'll tell you a story, instead."

She took a large gulp of wine and leaned forward, resting her arms on the table.

"A long time ago, in a land far away, a little girl lived with her mother and father in a peaceful village in the forest. Her mother was a Druid Priestess, her father a handsome warrior. They lived a life of tranquillity and happiness.

"Then one day, a Roman Centurion led his forces into our village. They burned and slaughtered and took the girl and her mother captive. She was very sad because the Romans had killed her father, and her grandfather. Also, she didn't like being a slave.

"The girl and her mother were taken to the Centurion's villa where they were put to work. It was a hard life, and the girl's mother kept trying to escape. She wanted to run away, back to her people, and she always took the girl with her.

"Running was hard, as well, and in the end, they were always caught. The woman was whipped, but then she would try again. It wasn't until the Centurion threatened to whip the girl that her mother stopped running. And so, they settled and, like good slaves, accepted their fate, worked hard, and stayed out of trouble."

"Is this a parable to encourage us too not be so troublesome?" Charlie asked.

Kayla smiled and drank deeply from her cup. "You could say that."

Then she glanced over her shoulder at the setting sun and continued.

"Life became easier after that," she said, "but the girl was still unhappy because she was still a slave. And the Centurion didn't forget the trouble her mother had caused, so he sent them away, to do farm labour, and life got hard once again. They lived in a tiny room by a brook, with the other slaves, and worked from sun to sun. The mother's beauty faded, and the girl grew sadder and sadder.

"But then the gods smiled. The mother caught the eye of the farm's overseer. They married. She and the girl moved into the villa. They wore fine clothing, ate good food, bathed, and enjoyed their time. And the girl kept the slave hut, turning it into her own little home. A slave—a farm slave—with her own house, a respected position, a beautiful mother, a pliable stepfather, and a life of ease. The girl was happy once more, and stopped dreaming of running away."

The sun was low now, brushing the tops of the distant trees. Kayla remained silent. I looked into her eyes. "And then we showed up, right?"

She put her goblet down and leaned forward again. Her smile disappeared. "Mother thinks you've been sent by the gods to save our people. Lucius thinks you've been sent to make him a rich man. And I think you've been sent to take all this away from me." As she said it, she swung her arm around to indicate the farm and the villa, and nearly unseated herself. She took another long drink.

"So let us go," Charlie said.

Kayla settled. "I want to, we want to, mother and I. We begged Lucius, but he remains unmoved. He will not let you go."

Then she looked at us and smiled, and my stomach grew cold.

"But he doesn't have to keep you here. He has an uncle, an overseer in an iron mine in Cantiaci. He has sent a runner to arrange for your transport. By this time tomorrow, you will be down in a mineshaft, safely out of sight, safely off this farm, and the girl can go back to being happy."

I felt the blood drain from my face. I wanted to say something, anything, but I couldn't speak.

"And what about us?" Charlie asked. His voice sounded small.

Kayla laughed and flung her arm out behind her,

drawing our attention to the sun, half-hidden behind the distant trees.

"Have a good look," she said. "It's the last sunset you'll see for a long, long time."

Chapter 11

"Three years!"

Lucius nodded as he unhitched the horse. "Don't worry, it will go by fast enough."

"In the dark?"

He shrugged, leading the horse away from the wagon. "That's what mines are. Dark."

He seemed unnaturally cheerful about it. But then he was getting what he wanted, and we certainly weren't.

We'd spent a largely sleepless night, first trying to find a way to escape, then, when it got too dark to see, trying to think of a way to escape, and finally, as morning came, frantically searching for a way to escape. We thought we had a few hours to work something out, because Kayla had gleefully informed us that we would be gone by the following afternoon, shipped off to Lucius's uncle's mine, where we would toil night and day in perpetual darkness—comfortably out of sight—until Fabianus granted Lucius his freedom and he could safely take possession of us. So, we were surprised when, after only half an hour into our morning search, Lucius came to take us to the field.

Charlie protested that it wasn't fair. If we were to be sent to the mines, he reasoned, we shouldn't be expected to work the fields. But Lucius had replied, saying, "You are slaves. Slaves work."

He hitched a wagon and he and Titus drove us to the same field we had worked in the previous two days, while we laid in the back of the cart, hiding from the other slaves. It wasn't until we got to the field and Lucius prepared to leave that I had asked him how long we would be working for his uncle.

His response made me feel faint. We hadn't expected to be taken to the field, so we had left our money in the bathhouse, and I hadn't expected to be working in the mine for that long. How would we ever get our cloak back? And what about the money?

"What if we promise to cooperate?" I asked. "We could work for you and stay out of sight."

Lucius shook his head. "You were right. There is no way word of you would not get out. And if Fabianus found I had taken two slaves instead of giving them to him, things would go very badly for me."

"Way to go, Mitch," Charlie said. "Making him see sense."

My stomach twisted into knots, and I felt like throwing up the small meal of mush we'd had for breakfast.

"You two and Titus make a good team," Lucius said, leading the horse away. "You should have that wagon filled before my messenger returns. Then I can send you on your way."

We watched him go, heading for the lane that led back to the villa.

"I am sorry this happened," Titus said. He looked like he meant it.

"We could run now," Charlie said.

Titus nodded. "I would be branded, and even if I was willing to suffer that for you, you would still go to the mine. Each without a foot."

Charlie scuffed at the dirt. "So, what do we do now?"

"I find work helps ease a troubled mind," Titus said. He was still looking at Lucius, who was just about to disappear behind the trees. Then he stood straighter. "A runner comes. There is news."

My stomach lurched. I leaned over, preparing to see my breakfast again.

The runner was Cassius. He shouted something to Lucius, who turned and began running toward us.

"I do not think this is good news," Titus said. "Lucius looks troubled."

"He should try some hard work, then," Charlie said.

Lucius drew nearer, the horse trotting at a quick pace behind him.

"Fabianus is coming," he shouted. "Quick, into the cart."

Lucius and Titus hitched the horse in record time and soon we were bouncing around in the back, trying to remain prone on the boards. It was a painful, though short, journey.

Back in the farmyard, Lucius pulled to a juddering stop in front of the bathhouse. Then he jumped from the cart and grabbed us each by an arm.

"Inside," he said, hauling us out of the cart and pushing us through the open door. It slammed behind us, and the bolt slid home.

Charlie kicked at the door. "What? Does he expect us to just sit in here nice and quiet and stay hidden for his sake?" He kicked the door harder. "We should raise holy hell. If he's so afraid of Fabianus, maybe we should make sure he finds us." He looked at me. "Or do you have a better idea?"

There was something about his plan that didn't set

well with me, but I had to admit I didn't have anything else to suggest. The only thing I thought of that he didn't was the money.

"We need to find a way to hide these on us," I said, as I dug the two bags out of the pool.

Our tunics didn't have any pockets, and there was nothing to tie them to except the leather belt, which was outside. We tried sticking them in our underwear, but they were too heavy. They just pulled our underwear down, then flopped out at our feet. Not a good solution.

"We could hang them around our necks," Charlie suggested.

I thought that might work. The only problem was, we didn't have any twine. I looked at the blankets, but they were tightly woven. The discarded Roman underwear looked like a better bet. I couldn't unravel it, but I could tear it. I made a start using the sharp edge of one of the rocks sticking out of the wall, then tore off a strip of fabric. It made a good loop that I hung around my neck, with the bag of coins near my waist. By blousing out the tunic around my middle, it hid it well enough.

I made a second loop for Charlie, and we had just finished blousing his tunic when the latch clicked. I froze, not knowing what I feared most—Fabianus finding us, or Lucius returning to say we could now go to his uncle's mine. But, instead of either of them, the door flew open, and Kayla rushed in. Her hair was down and dishevelled, and she wore a tunic similar to ours that, after the fine clothing I was used to seeing her in, looked odd.

"Get out!" she shouted. "Now."

I turned to her, startled. "What?"

"Is this a trick?" Charlie asked.

"No," she said. "Go. Run."

"But Lucius," I said, "he told us—"

"Lucius is a fool," she said, snatching up our blankets and kicking up the hay we had flattened by sleeping on it. "He has no idea of what it is like to despise being a slave. He thinks you'll sit quietly in here until Fabianus goes away. And even if you're too stupid to raise a racket, he's bound to look in here."

"Well," Charlie said, "now that you mention it, we sorta figured we'd try that."

"As would I," she said, looking around. "So, go. Who knows how long Fabianus will remain here. You could be in the next district by the time anyone looks for you. You might even get away."

"Then let's go," Charlie said.

I nodded, "This could be our only chance."

Charlie ran out of the bathhouse, and I followed, the bag of coins bouncing against my stomach.

"To the house," I said. "We need the cloak."

We ran toward the villa, with Kayla chasing after us. "Not that way. Go toward the fields. You're going to run right into them."

We ignored her, ran to the door of the villa, pulled it open and rushed inside.

"What do you think you're doing?" Kayla called. "Get out of there."

The interior of the villa was so opulent I paused for a moment. The floors were tiled with pictures and intricate designs. The walls were painted bright colours—yellow, orange, blue—and had fancy tapestries and pictures hanging on them. Unlit oil lamps hung from the ceiling, and sunlight streamed in through open windows. Couches with puffy cushions

75

were arranged around the room, along with tables and bureaus and chairs that were so delicately made they looked modern.

"This way," Charlie said.

We ran from the big room we were in, which must have been what we might call a reception room, through an open archway into another room with more couches and cushions and chairs, and into another with a bed and big wooden box.

"Try in there," I said.

"Keep out of that," Kayla shouted.

Charlie threw the lid up. We flung the garments out. No cloak.

We ran to the next room, but Kayla was almost on us.

Charlie opened another box as Kayla grabbed me around the neck.

"No cloak," Charlie said, when all the garments were scattered around the room.

"Leave that alone," Kayla said.

Charlie ran into the next room as I struggled with Kayla. "Hey," he called. "I found out why they're using that bathhouse to store hay. And there are cabinets in here. Maybe the cloak is in one. Keep her occupied."

Kayla gripped me in a headlock. "Get out of there."

"Oops, one fell in the pool," Charlie said. "And another."

"Don't you do that," Kayla said. "Don't you dare do that."

"Then give us our cloak," I said.

Kayla let out a frustrated scream and let me go.

I ran toward Charlie. Kayla ran the other way.

The room looked like I imagined our prison had before they filled it with hay. There was a shallow pool, surrounded by a floor of decorative tiles. The windows were long rectangles situated up high, probably, I reasoned, to let light in and keep the breezes out. Charlie stood near an open chest, with garments and blankets heaped around it. I was glad to see he hadn't really thrown them in the pool.

"It's not here," he said. "This way."

We ran into the next room. Unlike the rest of the house, it was unfinished, with stone blocks piled near the blank walls and a wooden bucket with sand in it.

"There's nothing here," I said. "Let's try the next one."

Then I heard Kayla rushing up behind me. I thought she was going to get me in a headlock again, but she thrust something at me, almost knocking me down.

"Here," she said. "Now go."

It was our cloak. I bundled it under my arm. "We need our clothes."

"I'll get your clothes," she said, pulling open a cabinet and taking out a broom. I jumped aside as she swung it at me. "Get out."

We ran into the next room, and the next, with Kayla swinging the broom behind us.

"There's a door ahead," Charlie said.

"No, not that one," Kayla shouted.

We ran toward it, barrelling through, with Kayla close behind. Then we stopped and Kayla ran into my back.

The front of the house had a paved courtyard with a semi-circular drive reaching to the road that I assumed led to Horsham. Lucius was there, with Ameena beside him. Standing with them were twenty or so men, women, and children. They were watching a group of chestnut horses trotting down the circular driveway. Mounted on the horses were soldiers. Roman soldiers.

"By the gods, we're in it now," Kayla said. "That's Fabianus."

Chapter 12

The soldiers, wearing helmets and breastplates of polished bronze that glinted in the sun, trotted into the courtyard in single file, then lined up facing Lucius, Ameena, and the group of slaves. Most of the soldiers wore short, broad swords at their sides, and two carried lances. The soldier on the lead horse, who wore a larger sword, an ornate breastplate, and a red cape, positioned himself in front of the others. His leather sandals were laced up to his knees and on his head was a helmet with a curved brush on top sprouting red bristles.

Lucius turned our way and went white. Ameena also looked at us, but she showed no fear, only resignation.

When the last of the horses joined the line, the soldier on the lead horse sat straight in his saddle and took a long, slow look around, as if he was surveying his domain, which, if he was Fabianus, I guess it was. He looked to the distant trees, then at the people gathered in front of him, giving special attention to Lucius and Ameena. Then he looked at us, giving us each a lengthy appraisal before turning back to Lucius.

"Lucius," he said. "This is a strange turn. I have come to interrogate you on why you have not sent my tribute, but now I wish to know why I do not recognize these two young slaves."

"Fabianus," Lucius said, his voice strained. "I—"

"We're not slaves," Charlie said.

Fabianus inclined his head in our direction. "Then why are you dressed as slaves."

"We're travellers," I said. "We stopped here, to rest, and Lucius was kind enough to give us lodging, and food."

"And make you his slaves?"

"No," I said. "We are repaying his kindness, um, by working. We didn't want to get our clothes dirty."

"And this house slave is chasing you, supposed free men, with a broom?"

"I just swept," Kayla said, "and they were tracking dirt over my clean floor."

Fabianus turned to Lucius. "You have sent no tribute this season, and yet you are spending money on construction. And you seem to have bought two slaves for yourself, without consulting me."

"Fabianus, I never—"

"We are not slaves," I said. "We're just travellers. And we are leaving now."

Fabianus smiled. "Are you? Or are you common thieves, stealing from your supposed benefactor? What is that you are holding?"

"A cloak," I said. "It's ours."

"I would see this cloak," Fabianus said. "Captain Remus, relieve them of it."

One of the soldiers dismounted and strode toward us. He was a big man, broad in the shoulders, with a scruffy, black beard and a fearsome look on his face. He pulled the cloak from my hands, took it to Fabianus and handed it up to him.

"An interesting, and expensive, garment," Fabianus said, unfurling it. "And you say it is yours?"

"Yes," I said. "Our grandfather gave it to us."

"It was a gift," Charlie added.

"A generous gift," Fabianus said, running his hand over the material. "From where did you travel?"

I looked at Charlie. "Wynantskill."

Fabianus shook his head. "I have been the length and breadth of this land, and I know of no Wynantskill. I hold that you are common thieves, or slaves stealing from their master. Either crime merits execution."

I felt the blood drain from my face and felt faint. Charlie, too, went white. I opened my mouth to speak but couldn't find the words. Then Ameena came to us and put a hand on my shoulder. "The prophecy is being fulfilled," she said, her voice low and urgent. "Promise me, whatever transpires, that you will care for my daughter."

"But … he wants to kill us," I said.

Ameena smiled. "Have no fear. Just promise."

I nodded my head. "We do, don't we, Charlie."

Charlie gulped and nodded.

"These boys speak true," she said, turning to Fabianus. "They came to the farm. We provided shelter for them, and food. The cloak belongs to them."

All true, I thought, with only a few, minor details left out.

Fabianus looked at her, his dark eyes narrowing. "Your words strain credibility. But there is no uncertainty in the matter of my tribute."

"We are harvesting a good crop," Lucius said, "we merely need to wait for the prices to rise. The money will come."

Fabianus shook his head. "Money in the future does me no good. Or you. If you have none to give, I will take it."

"But Fabianus," Lucius pleaded, "a month, maybe

81

two, that is all—"

"No more excuses," Fabianus said, pointing beyond Lucius, to the people who were now clustered in a tight group. "Captain Remus, separate seven of the slaves. Send them to the market in Londinium. Take the woman and the girl, as well."

Lucius fell to his knees. "Fabianus, please, I beg you."

"And flog this wretch. If he begs again, take off the woman's head."

To her credit, Ameena didn't flinch. She stood, solemn, watching her husband beg.

"Cato, Gaius," Captain Remus shouted, "with me."

Two soldiers dismounted, one with a short beard, weathered skin, and thick arms, the other clean-shaven with skin the colour of copper. The only thing they had in common was the cold and unyielding expression on their faces. They marched with Captain Remus into the group of cowering slaves and began pulling children from their mothers, and husbands from their wives. The crying and pleading made my stomach wrench.

"Why are you doing this?" I shouted.

"Shut up, Mitch," Charlie hissed.

Fabianus looked at me, shocked. "Have this one whipped, as well."

The fear left me. All I felt was rage. "This is cruel. There must be some other way."

Fabianus laughed. "Unless you have the money to pay this man's tribute, there is no other way. Captain Remus, flog him."

Remus released the struggling woman he was holding and, grinning, came my way.

I pulled the bag of coins from my tunic and held it up. "I have money. So does my brother. We will pay, just don't whip anyone. And don't send anyone away."

Fabianus held up his hand. Captain Remus stopped, Cato and Gaius released the people they were holding. The cries of the slaves gradually eased. "You have money? You would pay this man's tribute?"

I nudged Charlie. "Yes, we will," I said.

Charlie pulled his coins out of his tunic and held the leather bag up. Fabianus glared at us. "Come, let me see what you offer."

Charlie and I walked forward. When we got to his horse, Fabianus grabbed the bag from my hand and opened it to peer inside.

"There is, indeed, a great deal of money here." He grabbed Charlie's coins and inspected them. "This is too much for two vagabonds to steal. Where did you get this?"

"Our grandfather," I said. "He gave it to us. Along with the cloak."

Fabianus looked again at the coins. Then he put the bags in a pouch hanging from his belt. "Your grandfather must be a wealthy man to give you this much money so you could tour the Empire."

"He is," I said. "And generous."

"And reckless," Fabianus said. "Two boys, travelling alone, with such a treasure. I am surprised you were not set upon."

"We can take care of ourselves," Charlie said.

Fabianus nodded. "So I see. You are noble and brave, but foolish. Do not think you will win the favour of a man like Lucius with this gesture. He turned to Remus, who was still holding a woman and a young boy. "Release them. And leave Lucius unharmed."

Lucius bowed his head. "Thank you. Thank you."

"You are not yet released," Fabianus said. "This

83

money buys you a month, that is all. On the next moon, you will take the harvest to the markets in Noviomagus. All you earn will be delivered to me at my villa. If I judge it to be sufficient, I will let you return to your wife."

"Thank you," Lucius said again, his head still bowed.

"As for you," Fabianus said, looking down at us. "I cannot allow you to continue on such a perilous journey without protection. It would be doing your grandfather a disservice. You will come with me, as my guests. I will send word to your grandfather and bring you safe to him. I expect to find him, as you have remarked, generous."

I nodded, inwardly cringing. "You will."

"And I will see that your cloak remains safe. For your benefit, of course."

Of course, I thought.

"Our grandfather would want the cloak to stay with us," Charlie said.

Fabianus made no reply, and instead turned to the soldiers behind him. "We leave now. There is a full day's march ahead and the sun is already high."

Captain Remus returned to his horse, but before he mounted, Fabianus called to him. "Bring the girl."

Lucius raised his head, but Ameena, who had returned to his side, put a hand on his shoulder and he said nothing.

Fabianus ordered the slaves to bring a horse and cart. It didn't take long, and soon the three of us—me, Charlie, and an enraged Kayla—were bundled into the back. One of the soldiers tied his horse to the rear of the cart and took the driver's seat, flicking the reins to make the cart-horse jump. The paved courtyard was smoother than the farm lanes so—even as the cart lurched forward—the bumping and rattling wasn't as bad, and it made it possible to hear Ameena call to us as we turned onto the Horsham road.

"Remember your promise."

I looked her way and nodded once. Then she disappeared from view.

Chapter 13

We didn't head toward town. Instead, we left the villa behind and travelled in the opposite direction.

"Where is he taking us?" Charlie asked.

"To his villa," Kayla said, "outside of Noviomagus Regnorum, where I was a house slave years ago." Then she glared at us. "You've just stolen the best years of my life."

I could have said it wasn't our fault. I could have pointed out that she had chased us into the courtyard. I could have reminded her that we hadn't wanted to be on her farm in the first place. But she didn't seem in the mood for that sort of conversation. Charlie, too, was quietly sulking, sitting in the far corner of the cart.

Wherever we were heading, we were making good time. The road was broad and flat, and the few people we encountered had to scurry out of our way as the soldiers, with Fabianus in the lead—already wearing our cloak—trotted on unimpeded. I watched fields and woodlands and expansive pastures—where horses and cattle grazed—glide by, wondering if we had improved our situation or put ourselves in greater danger.

"At least this time we're riding in a cart with a horse trailing behind us," I said to Charlie, in an attempt to cheer him up, "instead of running behind the horses."

"But just like last time, we're prisoners," he said, "and our cloak has been stolen."

I took a deep breath, determined to avoid an argument. We weren't heading for the mines, no one had been whipped, we were not in immediate danger, and the cloak was, I felt certain, where it was supposed to be.

"Remember what the Druid told us," I said. "The cloak and the Talisman want to be together. We know who has the cloak, so we know where it, and the Talisman, are."

Charlie grunted and looked away, but Kayla lifted her head. "Druid? And what do you mean, 'this time'? Were you here before?"

I nodded. "But in a different time."

"Of course it was a different time," she said. "When?"

"Depends. What's the date today?"

"It's the fifth year of the reign of Emperor Aurelian. The Mothers' Moon is not a week passed, and we are entering the cycle of the Horse Moon."

Charlie gave a disgusted snort. "Well, that clears things up."

I struggled to recall anything I knew about the Roman Empire. It was big around the time Jesus was born. Were we beyond that time? And when were we here last? I'd done some research on King Arthur in the days after we'd returned from our last adventure. That wasn't exactly straightforward, but I did find a supposed date when he supposedly died, which was sometime in the 500s, and that put us a long way from Jesus, so I assumed, in her world, our first visit was somewhere in the future.

"It was in a very different time," I said to Kayla. "Hundreds of years different."

She shook her head. "That's not possible."

I shrugged. "I agree," I said. "But here we are."

Kayla didn't pursue the subject, and Charlie resumed his sulking, so I turned my attention back to the scenery.

About fifteen minutes later, the road we were on intersected with another road. It too was paved and flat and straight, but it was wider. In the area around the intersection, there were buildings, and people. Structures too large to be houses sat some way from the road, with pathways leading to them, and between them. Soldiers, men wearing robes, and even some women, walked the narrow lanes. There was a lot of activity, but it didn't appear to be a village. It was more like a school campus, or a military base.

It was there that we were joined by nearly thirty more people—some wearing military attire and others, like us, dressed in simple tunics. They had been waiting near the intersection for us and fell into step as we turned the corner to head down the wider road. The mounted soldiers rode in front with Fabianus, while the horse-drawn carts filed in behind.

We stopped for a few minutes to allow the soldier driving our cart to retrieve his horse and ride ahead to be with the others, leaving our cart in the care of the other drivers. There was talk of abandoning it, or sending it back to Lucius, but in the end, they decided to keep it because some of the other carts were over-loaded. They heaved bundles of slate, a few coils of coarse rope, and several large, two handled jugs, which Kayla called amphorae, into our cart, tying them down under a tarp. This meant we had to squeeze together in the back of the cart, forcing me to sit with my legs pulled up against my chest, knee-to-knee with Kayla, who kept throwing hateful looks my way because she couldn't turn far enough to give hateful looks to Charlie, who was pressed up against her side. A soldier climbed in with us, but he sat on the tarp with his back to the driver. I assumed he was our guard because, although he seemed bored and hardly ever looked at us, his hand never left the hilt of his sword.

"Move on," one of the drivers shouted. "We have far to go."

The company rode on. Soldiers, carts, wagons, and pack horses. It was hot and dusty and uncomfortable, but at least being packed in so tightly kept me from bouncing around.

I avoided Kayla's gaze by watching the scenery, which was difficult because I had to turn my head, and even then, all I could see was the road behind us, filled with horses and carts and dust. What little I could see was of gently rolling hills and grassland. It reminded me of the land we had travelled through the first time we had used the cloak. I thought about asking Charlie what he thought about it, but he didn't seem in the mood for conversation yet.

We rode for a long time, until the sun was high, then stopped for a quick lunch of bread, wine and soft cheese that smelled like feet. Charlie and Kayla still weren't talking, so the meal was eaten quickly and silently. About half an hour later we were moving again.

In the afternoon, the land became wooded, and the soldiers rode in tight formation, and the carts kept close, with trios of armed soldiers riding alongside them. Even our guard looked uncharacteristically alert. I watched the woods, then craned my neck to look at the soldiers, wondering why they seemed so wary.

"Celts," Kayla said. "They fear an attack."

I looked to the woods. The trees weren't thick, and no shadows moved among the low bushes.

"I don't see anyone."

"You won't," she said. "Not until it's too late." Somehow, she managed to make this sound like a threat.

The forests stretched on for miles. About two hours later, the trees became sparse, and the low bushes gave way to grassland. Now the terrain was flat, allowing a view of distant fields, an occasional cluster of houses and, once—on a rise not far from the road—another villa, much grander than Kayla's home. Or, her old home, I reminded myself.

We travelled through the afternoon and into the evening, as the sun dipped low in the sky. Assuming the 'Cycle of the Horse Moon' meant June, the days would be long, so it had to be well after dinner time. I wondered how long we were going to have to ride. Then, in the distance, I saw what looked like a huge wall. It was tall and thick and made of stone, and had turrets spaced along it at even intervals, like a medieval fortress.

As we drew near, I heard the soldiers and the other drivers mention the name Noviomagus Regnorum, the city Kayla had told us we were heading to. The villa wouldn't be far away.

The road we were on led into the city, rolling up to the walls at an oblique angle. There was an opening—a door or gate—set into the wall but, from my vantage point, I couldn't see inside. The sun was low, giving the walls an unnatural glow. As we drew nearer, I saw that the gate was guarded.

Charlie sat up straight and pointed over my shoulder. "What's that?"

With some difficultly, I turned around. The land outside the walls was trampled flat. There were pathways and a dirt track that seemed to lead around the city. And some distance away was an amphitheatre. I recognized it from the pictures I'd seen of Rome, but this one was smaller. Still, it was an impressive sight, and looked like it could hold a couple hundred people.

"It that the Coliseum?" Charlie asked.

"Yes," Kayla said without looking. "They hold games there."

"I thought that was in Rome."

"It's a coliseum," I said, "not the Coliseum. I expect every major city had something like that."

We had a good view of it as we approached the walls. It was impressive, but the most memorable thing was the smell. It wasn't a farm smell, it smelled more like something had gone rotten. No one else seemed to notice it, but Charlie and I wrinkled our noses.

At the wall, which towered above us, Fabianus greeted the guards, who stepped aside and let us through. We had to wait because, even though the gate was wide, the city street beyond it was narrower than the road, and we had to go single file. When our turn came and we passed through the thick walls, the smell changed from rotten to something more resembling an open sewer mixed with the less noxious smell of animal dung.

The city was crowded, which also made the going slow. There were people everywhere, many I judged to be slaves because they were dressed as we were, but there were also a large number of others, dressed in tunics of green, yellow, blue or the more common brown. The women wore long white dresses and had their hair piled on their heads in a manner that looked both complicated and uncomfortable. There were market stalls, where people haggled while flies buzzed around fish and meat. Added to that were the sounds of horse hooves clopping, wagons groaning, and hammering from somewhere nearby. The air was filled with dust and the smoke from dozens of small fires.

After turning the corner to get into the city, the road became straight, and through the line of mounted soldiers, carts, people, and the ever-present dust, I could see another gate, set into the western wall, not very far away. Unfortunately, the crowd of people— many of them stopping to stare at us or shout greetings, and all of them in our way—meant it took longer to get there than I would have liked.

Despite the stench, the city was surprisingly modern. The streets were laid out in a grid, and there was a large, open area in the centre, like a big town square. Next to that was an enormous bathhouse, and there were even public toilets, which we could smell more than see. Tiled drainage ditches on either side of the road carried brown sludge that oozed slowly toward the far wall where, I assumed, it was dumped into a cesspit.

Just when I seriously thought I might faint from the smell, we rolled through the opposite gate, into the less noisome scents of the countryside. Here the flat land was hard-packed and chequered with patches of grass. A few temporary huts and tents and carts were scattered across the field. Outside the tents, men tended fires and brought feed to their horses.

"It looks like a campground," Charlie said.

"Market," Kayla said, again without looking. "A temporary one. The next one will be at the full moon."

"Is this where your stepfather is coming to?" I

asked, hoping that getting her to talk might help her forget how angry she was.

"Lucius will be here," she said, "not that it will do him any good. He can never make enough money to satisfy Fabianus. After the market, he'll be executed, or taken to the slave auctions in Londinium. Along with mother."

It wasn't exactly turning into a cheery conversation, so I didn't pursue it.

"Lucky me, right?" Kayla said after a few moments of silence. "I get to go back to serving my master, in his huge and opulent villa. Back to my old life. Back to where I started."

I wasn't about to comment on that, but Charlie didn't seem to mind prodding her, which I thought was either brave or stupid, seeing as how he was right next to her. "I thought you started as a happy young girl living in your village in the woods."

Instead of hitting him, or even giving him a dirty look, Kayla hugged her knees and bowed her head. "A dream. I was young. I can never go back there."

"But you're closer to where you grew up now," Charlie said, "you could escape and go—"

"Silence," Kayla said, suddenly raising her head and turning to Charlie, their noses practically touching. "Such talk brings swift and unwelcome retribution. There is no escape. The Romans rule the world. There is no place to run to, unless you know of a land where the Romans do not exist."

"Well," Charlie said, losing interest in the conversation, "not here, I don't."

I turned away from them, looking again toward the front of our slow-moving column. About half a mile away, clearly visible on the flat terrain, and near where

93

a grey, shimmering ocean met the land, was a building I could only describe as a palace.

"Is that Fabianus's villa?" I asked, unable to keep myself from sounding awestruck.

Kayla, her forehead resting on her knees, nodded. "An opulent edifice," she said, "for a prison."

Chapter 14

I had expected another villa, like the one Lucius and Ameena lived in, or even like the one on the hilltop we had passed on our journey south, but comparing Fabianus's home to them was like comparing the Taj Mahal to a shack. And it didn't hurt that we had arrived when we did. The setting sun, which had given the walls of the city a pleasant radiance, made the palace—with its whitewashed walls and orange-tiled roof—glow.

The road led to an entrance hall that towered above the rest of the structure, its peaked roof supported by a row of majestic columns. From the entrance hall, the building stretched hundreds of feet—orderly and perfectly straight—in either direction, with a massive porch running the entire length of the lower level. Above the columned porch, a second tier, with a peaked, tiled roof, was set slightly back from the lower level. The walls were made entirely of stone and looked smooth as marble.

The area in front of the entrance hall was paved and guards stood by the giant wooden doors. They hailed Fabianus as he approached, and exchanged greetings and bits of news with the soldiers. The column did not stop there, however. It turned toward the ocean, following the paved courtyard to a track that led us along the front of the building, giving me a close-up view of the walls, the tiled roofs, and the windows, glazed with green-tinted glass.

At the back of the building, a broad strip of land separated the villa from the bay. Just beyond the edge of the track, a sandy, rock-strewn beach sloped toward the sea, where a wooden pier jutted into the harbour. A few small boats lay on the beach while others were tied up along the pier's edge, and at the far end, a square-rigged ship bobbed on the calm water.

As with the front side, a columned porch ran the length of the seaward wall, though at the near end, where we came to a stop, there was a huge, domed structure, belching smoke from a tall smokestack. Nearby, a broad opening led to a huge storeroom filled with stacks of lumber, bricks, roof tiles, buckets, and dozens of two-handled jugs like the ones we'd carried in our cart.

The soldiers dismounted and handed their horses to the men, women and boys streaming out to greet us. Others began unloading the carts and carrying the contents into the storeroom. Kayla, Charlie, and I stood together, not certain what to do. Then Fabianus approached, leading an older man with a stooped back and close-cropped white hair.

"Cenacus will see to you," Fabianus said. Then he looked at me and Charlie. "He will show you your apartment, where you will find proper clothes. Put them on. You are attending dinner as my guests. Cenacus, you have your orders."

Cenacus dipped his head low. "At your service." I figured that must have been where he got the stooped back from.

Fabianus turned to Kayla. "You. Follow."

Then he strode away, with Kayla following and our

cloak billowing out behind him. I watched her go, feeling a mixture of fear, regret, and sadness, and remembering the promise we had made to Ameena. Then I heard someone talking and realized it was Cenacus.

"You are the boys we were told about," he said, standing a little straighter. "Honoured guests of Fabianus. I will see to your comfort."

"Told about us?" Charlie asked.

Cenacus nodded. "A rider came some time ago with news of your approach. All is ready. You must come with me so you can change for dinner."

We followed him through the activity to another door that led into the villa. The hallway we entered was cavernous and glowing with light from the setting sun. We both stopped and stared.

"This is magnificent," Charlie said.

Cenacus grinned. "You have never seen a villa so opulent?"

"We've never seen a villa at all," I said.

Cenacus grunted. "They told us you were from a strange land. Come this way."

He led us down the hall, to where the domed building I had seen was. Instead of walking past, he pulled a set of double doors open and told us to follow. Moist heat enveloped us as soon as we stepped inside. The fading light provided little illumination where it filtered in through the high, narrow windows, but the interior was lit by dozens of oil lamps—the kind you might rub to make a genie appear—suspended from the ceiling by fine chains. The floor was a colourful mosaic of tiny tiles and much of the area was taken up by a large pool of steaming water. A few naked men, and women, were lounging in the water, resting against the sides, chatting amiably. Next to it was a smaller, round pool of clear water. I watched, amazed, as a man plunged into it, and emerged shivering and shaking. Nearby were stone tables, and a few people were lying on them while clothed men scraped their skin with curved knives.

"This is the bathhouse," Cenacus said, "the beating heart of the villa. Through those doors near the back are the furnaces, where all the hot water for the estate is heated and pumped to the rooms. The heated air is pumped into conduits under the floors to warm the villa in the winter.

We left the bathhouse through an arched door and entered a long hallway, which, like the bathhouse, allowed light in through windows set high in the walls, supplemented by lanterns fastened at intervals along the walls. The hall was wide, tall, and lavish, decorated with coloured wooden panels, tapestries, and intricate tiling. An open archway led to another, equally opulent, corridor and side rooms.

"These are storage rooms," Cenacus said, when he saw me looking. "Soldiers on guard duty stay in this wing. The rooms for my family and other guests are in the next wing, closer to the dining rooms and with access to the porticos surrounding the gardens."

When we came to the entrance hall, Cenacus said nothing; he let the room do the talking. It was vast, towering above us like a cathedral, its roof held in place by ornate columns and stone arches. With the doors barred for the night, the cavernous interior swallowed up the light from the torches and lanterns, leaving the grand hall looking dim and oppressive. In the centre of the room, looming out of the darkness like an apparition, stood an elaborate fountain. No water spouted from it, making it appear abandoned. As we crossed to the far side, our footsteps echoed, mingling with those of the soldier guards, unseen in the darkness.

We entered another corridor, and at the far end, Cenacus stopped outside an open door and ushered us into the room. Fading sunset and lanterns illuminated the interior, allowing us to see the bright colours of the walls, the wooden chest that looked remarkably like a dresser, the chairs, a table, and two beds, one on either side of the room. Near the back, an archway led to another, smaller room, containing a stone basin.

"You will stay here," Cenacus said. "You will find fresh clothes in the chest. The basin in the adjoining room will allow you a basic wash, but feel free to make use of the bathhouse. A meal is being prepared; you will be summoned to the dining hall when it is time. Until then, rest, and make yourselves comfortable."

I stared at the bed. It looked inviting, and it made me feel guilty, wondering where Kayla would sleep that night.

"What will happen to the girl who came with us?" I asked.

Cenacus sighed and smiled. "Yes, Kayla. She has grown so. It was a joy to see her. Thank you for returning her to us. Her mother was a mysterious and troubled woman, but Kayla had a spark. We all missed her when she was sent to be a farm labourer."

"Um, she did all right," Charlie said.

Cenacus bobbed his head. "I am pleased."

"Will she be treated well here?" I asked.

"As well as any of us." He looked around to be certain no one was listening at the door. "Fabianus can be cruel, but so can any master. He leaves the running of the villa to me. I will take good care of Kayla. She will have much lighter duties here than on the farm."

"I'm not sure about that," I said. "I hope she adjusts. It wasn't her idea to come with us."

"Slaves go where they are ordered," Cenacus said. "That is what we do." He started toward the door, then turned back. "You will be summoned to dinner soon, so be sure to get ready. And Fabianus has instructed me to tell you that it is dangerous to be outside the villa. There are guards on every door. If you wish to go outside, one of them will accompany you."

Then he left, closing the door behind him.

"Honoured guests," Charlie said, "or prisoners?"

I said nothing. The answer was obvious.

Chapter 15

In the late afternoon of our seventh day at the villa, while returning from the bathhouse to our apartment, we saw Kayla coming down the hallway toward us. We moved to the side, giving her a wide berth because she was still mad at us, and we were trying to avoid her. This time, however, she changed course and came straight toward us. There was no one else in the corridor and I wasn't sure what to expect. She might spit at us or hit us with the tray she was carrying.

We'd first encountered her at the dinner Fabianus had invited us to. Cenacus had come to our room to escort us, leading us to a large room with low tables where a dozen men and women were laying down on their sides on mats. We were shown to a mat and, taking a cue from the others, laid down on our side, propped up with our elbows, facing the table. Fabianus had greeted us and introduced us as his guests, then largely ignored us. I think the purpose was to let everyone see us so they could help keep an eye on us.

The people at the table, from the conversations we could overhear, seemed to be high ranking soldiers and civilians who worked at the villa. Captain Remus was among them, in civilian dress, reclining between two women. During the meal of quail, beef, pork, assorted vegetables, and fruits, we were quizzed by the other guests about who we were and where we were from.

We gave vague answers and tried to discourage any more questions.

As the servers came and went, I saw, to my chagrin, that Kayla was among them, dressed now in the same tunics the other slaves wore. She studiously avoided us, and I tried, out of embarrassment, to not look her way. The next morning, however, when we were led to a smaller, more private dining room for breakfast, she was there again, and there was no way to avoid her, or her us. She slammed our plates down in front of us and stalked out of the room, leaving me with little appetite. When we left the dining room to return to our apartment, we found her cleaning our room. When she saw us, she scowled, stopped what she was doing and walked to the door.

"I'm sorry," I said as she walked away, "but none of this is our fault."

"I miss my mother," she said, turning to face us. "And I want to go home."

"So do we," I said. "We might not be slaves, but we're prisoners here just like you."

"Some prison," she said, stomping out of the room. Then she paused at the door. "Enjoy it while you can. Fabianus is only pampering you because he thinks he can get a reward from your grandfather." Then she smiled. "He's sent riders out to find this Wynantskill you say you came from. Once they come back and tell him it doesn't exist, and that you don't have a grandfather, you'll be lucky if he merely makes galley slaves of you."

That gave us a lot to think about. We needed to find the cloak as soon as possible and somehow get back to the farm so we could return home. And, since we didn't have anything else to do, we made that our

102

mission.

Searching the villa was no easy feat. There were guards everywhere, and we had to be careful we weren't seen sneaking into any rooms. One day, we found the soldier's quarters, and on another we crept up a wooden stairway to the second floor, where the hallway was narrow and the rooms small and barren.

"This must be the slaves' quarters," Charlie said. "He wouldn't hide the cloak here."

Still, we returned time and again, when it was quiet, and searched a few rooms, all of them nearly empty and none of them hiding our cloak.

There were so many rooms off the north, south and east corridors we couldn't keep them straight, or search all of them. And there were some areas we couldn't get into because guards were posted outside the doors.

The west corridor was different because it was under construction.

As opulent and orderly as the other wings were, that one was cluttered and chaotic. The walls and the floors were covered with woven straw mats to protect them, and setting on the mats were buckets of tar, stacks of wood, and tiles. On the bare floor, which looked like concrete, sat a number of hollowed stone containers with smoke rising from them. There were also a lot of people, workmen, laying tiles, mixing sand and water in big metal cauldrons, carrying lumber, and climbing up and down ladders. It looked interesting, but we didn't want to be in the way—and there was obviously no place to hide our cloak there—so we turned to go back to the south corridor. Then someone called to us.

It was Cenacus, there to check on how the work was progressing, and he seemed eager to show it off to us.

"This is to be the new bathing area," he told us. "A

new type of bathhouse, larger, more open and encompassing the outdoors as well as the indoors. I designed it myself, at the request of Fabianus." He seemed pleased with himself, and the progress being made, and proceeded to give us an enthusiastic tour.

The pool was large, nearly as wide as the hallway itself, which had been enlarged to accommodate it. A grand entranceway in the newly built wall opened onto the central gardens, and the opposite wall was simply a gap, opening onto another, equally large pool outside the villa. About twenty men were working on ornate mosaics in and around the pools. A smell of harsh smoke hung in the air.

Cenacus led us into the empty pool, taking us down the slope from the shallow end to where the deep end stopped at the outer wall. Here, a pair of tunnels connected the two pools. "The new furnace at the edge of the garden will pump hot water into the outdoor pool," he said. "These tunnels will circulate the water, making it agreeable to swim, either inside or outside, winter or summer."

Several men were sitting—stooped and cross-legged—in the tunnels, tiling the curved walls.

He then led us back to the hallway and through an opening in the wall to the outside pool, which was protected by an extension of the porch. Its peaked roof was covered in the same, orange tiles as the rest of the villa but there was a bare strip between the villa and the new porch where half a dozen men were busy nailing down strips of wood and pouring what looked like hot tar over it.

"The seam will be closed up soon," Cenacus said, when he saw me looking. "They are skilled tilers. When the work is finished, you will not guess they were ever apart."

The roofing was demanding work, and Cenacus wanted to impress that on us. The tiles, which he called terracotta, were laid down in overlapping rows, stuck down with tar, but it wasn't tar made from petroleum, like I figured it was. That had made sense to me, because if the Romans owned the whole world, they certainly had access to oil, but when I mentioned this, Cenacus gave me a quizzical look and told me it was made from birch bark.

He then showed us one of the stone heaters with a metal cauldron hanging over it. Inside was a hot, dark liquid that didn't smell of gasoline, but instead had a sweet, leathery—and strangely familiar—scent mixed with the harsher scent of burnt wood. It was kept hot, Cenacus told us, to keep it in liquid form so the boys could carry buckets of it up the ladders to the men on the roof. The tiles were stuck down with the tar as it cooled, and the seams sealed with molten lead to make them waterproof. The lead, also kept hot in stone furnaces in the hallway, was carried to the roof by slaves who were skilled at working with hot metal.

"The work is progressing well," he said, as we ended the tour, "and ahead of schedule because, I insist on keeping the fires going throughout the night. That way, when the work begins in the morning, the tar and lead are already hot and ready for the roofers." He seemed inordinately proud of this, and I had to admit, it was an impressive operation, and not something I would have imagine possible for such an ancient civilization.

The baths, too, were impressive. It took us a while to try them, but after scrambling around in storerooms and attic spaces, we were soon too dirty to get clean by just using our sink, so one afternoon, we went to the bathhouse. It was a little awkward at first, because everyone was naked. Even the slaves wore very little. I think they had to wear something to show they were slaves, but they wore as little as possible because it was so hot in there. Strangely, it soon became more embarrassing to be wearing clothes because everyone else wasn't, so we stripped off and sat in the pool and soon felt a lot more at ease, not to mention cleaner.

The only thing I didn't like was the cold plunge after the bath, but it seemed to be expected of us, so we did it, then laid on the warm stone tables while barely dressed slaves, men, and women, scraped the water and sweat off us with dull, curved blades. It was so pleasant we began going every afternoon.

There were always people there. Mostly women, wives of the men working for Fabianus, but the higher-ranking slaves also enjoyed the baths. We saw Cenacus there a few times, and even Captain Remus, though we stayed well clear of him. We also saw Kayla there, but on those occasions, we didn't stay. It wasn't just because she was mad at us; being naked with Kayla, while she, herself, was naked, might be … well, I just didn't think it would be a good idea. So, if we saw her among the women, we quietly slipped away before she noticed us, returning to take our usual place in the pool only after we were certain she had left.

It was by visiting the baths that we heard the rumours about us, sometimes in whispers, other times by being asked point blank. Were we the sons of a senator, or pretenders and thieves? Were we wise men disguised as boys and sent by the gods? Were we destined to bring wealth and prosperity to the villa, or had we come to prophesy its destruction? We did our best to assuage their fears and gain their confidence,

106

and in doing so, we were kept informed of the progress of the messengers—the runners and riders Fabianus had sent throughout the countryside—searching for Wynantskill and a grandfather who didn't exist. It wasn't comforting news. They told us, if Fabianus found no proof of who we claimed to be, we would likely be executed or, if we were lucky, sent to sea as galley slaves. When they told us this, we smiled and tried to convey confidence that proof would certainly be found.

After bathing and dressing, we went to dinner, where too often we would be served by Kayla, who continued to glare at us and accidentally spill drinks on our clean clothes.

And this was why, when we encountered her in the deserted hallway, and she appeared to be coming our way, I felt a certain amount of trepidation. But she didn't try to hit us, or spit at us, or even look our way. She just walked by, saying, in a quiet voice as she passed us: "Sunset. North portico. I've found your cloak."

Chapter 16

Sunset wasn't until about nine thirty, so we had a lot of time to fill after dinner. We didn't want to hang around on the porch that long, fearing it might raise suspicion, so we did what we usually did, which was wander around the hallways, poking our noses into random rooms looking for our cloak. Because we weren't really searching, we soon grew tired of that, so we went to the north corridor to see how the construction was coming along.

Being late, there wasn't much activity, but there were still workmen there, tiling in the dying light and tending the fires still burning in the miniature stone furnaces. Cenacus wasn't there, but we recognized some of the workers. As usual, guards were standing at the openings, making sure no one came in or out who wasn't supposed to. And that included us.

It occurred to me that there was one opening they weren't guarding, and that was the connecting tunnels between the pools. They were easily big enough for a man to swim through, but Cenacus had told us that, once the pools were finished, the indoor pool would be covered at night, so anyone trying to sneak in that way would be trapped and drowned. A simpler solution would have been to fasten a grate over the openings, but I think Fabianus liked the idea of drowning people, rather than just discouraging them.

When we had wandered around long enough, we went to the northern corridor and out onto the porch. It was still light, and very warm, and people—residents, off-duty soldiers, and slaves—were strolling around in the internal gardens and lounging on the porch. It was a big porch, though, so we found a spot deep in shadow and well away from everyone and tried to look inconspicuous.

We waited a long time, until the light began to leave the sky, and we started believing we might have been tricked. Then we heard a voice from deeper in the shadows, near the villa.

"Over here."

It was Kayla, standing by the wall. We hadn't seen her approach, which struck me as odd because we had a full view in both directions. Charlie and I casually wandered over to her.

"Where is it?" Charlie asked. "Did you bring it?"

"Of course not," she said, keeping her voice low and her eyes on the other people on the porch and in the garden.

"But you do know where it is," I said.

She looked annoyed but nodded her head once. "Listen carefully. I'm going to walk away, and you will follow. But wait a few minutes. Don't let anyone suspect we're going off together."

With that, she turned and walked along the porch to a small door and went inside.

"Do you think she's lying?" Charlie asked.

"No," I said, "but I don't think she's telling the truth, either; not all of it, anyway."

"So, what do we do?"

"We don't really have a choice, do we?"

We waited a few minutes until we were sure no one

was watching, then we went to the small door, which was just a plain panel set into the wall. If you weren't looking for it, you'd never see it. We pulled it open and stepped inside.

It led to a cramped corridor where Kayla waited, holding a lantern. Despite all our exploring, we had never encountered anything like it.

"This is a service corridor," Kayla said. "The slaves use it to access the more important rooms, so they won't be seen going in and out of the main doors. Now keep silent and follow."

The corridor was low and narrow and smelled of damp, stale air—more like a tunnel than a hallway—so we had to walk single file. When I held my arms away from my sides, my fingers brushed the walls, which were rough stone festooned with cobwebs. I pulled my hands back and wiped them on my tunic.

We walked slowly, following the glow of Kayla's lamp. When she came to an intersection, she turned, then turned again, and shortly came to a dead end. She put her ear to the wall and listened for a moment, then pushed gently against it until a crack of light appeared.

"It looks safe," she said, peering through the opening. "Follow me. Quietly."

She pushed on the wall again. It swung open, and we stepped into a large room.

"This is Fabianus's apartment," she said, closing the door behind us. Like the door at the other end, it was a panel in the wall, invisible to anyone who didn't know it was there. "He's in a meeting but will be back soon. We must be quick."

The room was lavishly decorated with tapestries, ebony furniture, and a large mosaic of a battle scene—complete with blood-red tiles and depictions of severed limbs—in the centre of the floor in the main chamber. Not far from where we entered was a bed, its base and posts intricately carved into grape vines, and in the wall opposite was a niche, housing a marble bust of a man who looked suspiciously like Fabianus. Kayla led us into an adjoining room, with dressing tables, wardrobes, and tall chests with drawers. She set the lantern on a table, slid open the top drawer of one of the cabinets and carefully scooped out a small wooden box. We stared at it in disbelief.

"That's not our cloak."

"If you're trying to trick us—"

"Hush," Kayla said. "Your cloak is near, but first I have to show you this."

"All we want is our cloak," I said. "We don't want to see anything else."

"I think you do," Kayla said in a strangely calm voice. "I saw him this morning. He didn't know I had entered. He was wearing your cloak and holding … something."

"This box?" Charlie asked.

"No, the thing he keeps inside it," she said. "It unsettled me, the way he held it, the way he gazed into it, so I crept away. I knew if he caught me, he would be angry."

I took a quick look over my shoulder toward the door. "What are we waiting for? Show us so we can get out of here."

"I wish it were that simple," she said again, in that strangely resigned voice. "I fear what he keeps in this box is the sacred amulet he stole years ago. If it is, and if you truly are the travellers mother saw in her prophecy, then you must take this with you, and you must leave immediately, for he will know it is gone the moment you take it, and he will pursue you like a wolf, with great speed and savagery."

"Then take it, give us our cloak and let's get out of here."

She shook her head. "First, you must see it. We must be sure."

Kayla pushed a hidden latch on the bottom of the box, then slid one side up halfway and one end down, then the lid opened. "It's a puzzle box," she said. "You need to know the combination to open it. My mother had one like it. Look here." She held the box out. "Is this the Talisman?"

Inside the velvet lined box was a single object: a stone, disc-shaped, and so deeply black it looked like a hole through the cushion it was resting on. The smooth surface both reflected light, and drew it in. I looked closer, feeling a familiar pull. "Yes," I said. "That's the Talisman."

"Our legends say it came from the goddess Brighid, that it is a window, and a mirror, and that, when you hold it, and look into it, the gods show you things."

"Yes," Charlie said, his voice a mixture of impatience and panic, "that's how it works. Now let's go."

But Kayla continued staring into the box. "You have held it?"

"Yes," I said. "Have you?"

She shook her head slowly.

"But you want to?"

She nodded. "I confess I fear what I may see, but if you are the chosen—"

Charlie reached into the box and grabbed the stone. "Stop wasting time. Here, I'm holding it, I'm looking at it. I see my face, now can we …"

His face went slack. His jaw dropped. His eyes grew wide and white.

"Charlie, are you all right?" I asked.

"I see fire," Charlie said, his breath coming in short gasps as if he were inhaling the smoke. "It's everywhere. A tunnel of flames. I can't bre …"

I grabbed the stone from him, and he staggered backward, his face white. I looked down at the Talisman, now resting in my hand. It didn't take long. The slight pull I'd felt became a torrent. I tried to pull away, but the Talisman held me, even as the water rolled over me, dragging me under, threatening to choke me. "Water," I gasped. "I'm in water, I can't move, I'm drowning." My mouth opened but my breath stuck in my throat.

Somewhere in the distance, I heard Charlie's voice. "Help him."

I felt the stone leave my hand. The water disappeared. I took a breath and looked at Kayla, who was now holding the Talisman. Her eyes were wide with fear, but she looked down at the black disc in her hand. Charlie and I held our breath.

Slowly, her eyes focused, not on the Talisman, but on something beyond it. Her mouth became a perfect "O" and, instead of terror, her expression was one of puzzlement.

"I see my children," she said, "and their children, and their children's children. And from them, from me, a great king, a king who will unite Britannia, who will live in legend, who will save the Land …"

We watched her as she stared into the stone, all of us mesmerized and none of us knowing anything was amiss until a hand appeared, seemingly out of thin air, and plucked the Talisman from Kayla's grip.

"Perhaps you might like to know what I see," Fabianus said, "when I look into this trinket."

Chapter 17

My first instinct was to run, but then I thought, "Why bother?" Fabianus was blocking our way and, even if we could get around him, there was nowhere to run to. Kayla was right. We were trapped in the villa, and now trapped by Fabianus, who stood between us and the door, holding the Talisman, turning it slowly, staring into its dark surface.

"Shall I tell you what I see?" he asked, still looking at the stone. Then he lowered it and stared at each of us, individually, looking from Charlie, to me, then to Kayla, who still held the puzzle box. "What is this? Have the gods struck you dumb? You were chatting happily before I interrupted." He took the puzzle box from Kayla, laid the Talisman on the velvet pillow, and closed the box. "I see myself," he said, "dressed in the finest regalia, with people bowing at my feet, calling me Emperor."

He stepped around us, to the chest of drawers and put the puzzle box back where Kayla had found it. "Yes, the mirror shows this to me, my destiny, every morning, and every evening. I see it as clearly as I see you cowering in front of me. It has been written in the stars by the hands of the gods themselves." Then he opened another drawer, about halfway down, and took out what looked like a coiled-up leather belt. But it wasn't a belt. He let it uncoil, holding one, thick end, and letting the other dangle. There were several strands, strips of leather, with bits of jagged metal fixed to them. Charlie and I looked at it, puzzled. We had never seen anything like it before. But Kayla had. She turned white and ran.

Fabianus moved like a snake, quick and sharp, darting across the floor and grabbing Kayla before she was halfway across the bedchamber.

"You insignificant barbarian," he hissed. "I saw you spying on me. The stone told me what you were up to. I took you into my home and how do you repay me? You thought to better me, to steal my belongings." He pushed Kayla to the floor. "This is how I repay treachery."

Kayla rolled into a ball, holding her hands over her head, screaming, "No!"

Fabianus brought the lash down. Hard. Kayla screamed. The metal shards ripped her tunic and tore the flesh on her back. Another strike. More slashes. Kayla's cries filled the room, her tattered tunic turned red.

"No," Charlie shouted, but his voice was scarcely audible above Kayla's screaming.

"We've got to help her," I said.

The whip cracked again. Kayla howled and more blood flowed.

"Help her how?"

"I don't know, but we promised."

We rushed forward. Fabianus had his back to us, so we dove at him, hitting him in the back and the legs. Our momentum carried us all forward and we fell to the hard floor, with Fabianus thrashing and shouting beneath us. We sprang off and stood in front of Kayla and waited.

Fabianus climbed to his feet and picked up the whip, trailing it along the floor like a dead snake. "I was unsure of what to do with you two," he said, glaring down at us. "I knew you were lying the moment I saw you, but you had that cloak. I felt it was important, and now I know it is, and I thought, perhaps the gods put you in my path to assist in my rise to power. Now I see I was wrong. Once I affirmed there was truly no reward for helping you, I was merely going to sell you at the slave markets, but now you participate in this girl's treachery." He looked at the whip. "Yes. I think this is for you, as well."

The leather thongs whistled as he swung the whip over his head. All I could do was cross my arms in front of my face and close my eyes. My stomach turned to ice, and I felt like I was going to piss myself, or throw up, or both. I held my breath and waited. But nothing happened.

My ears buzzed. I thought I heard a voice. I drew a ragged breath and opened one eye. Captain Remus had entered the room. He seemed unconcerned about Kayla bleeding on the floor, and us cowering over her while Fabianus held a whip over his head. He didn't even look our way.

"Fabianus," he said, "I regret that I must interrupt."

Fabianus lowered the whip with a look of annoyance. "What is it that cannot wait?"

"A messenger awaits you in the Grand Hall. From the Senate."

Fabianus slowly coiled the whip. "I suppose I can finish this later," he said, "when I have leisure time to enjoy your pain." Then he turned to Captain Remus. "Lock them in the storeroom."

We helped Kayla to her feet, each of us holding an

arm as she hobbled along between us. The back of her tunic was in tatters and soaked with blood, but she didn't cry out. She walked as straight as she could, making only the occasional whimper.

We left by the main door and followed the corridor to the western wing, through the construction site and into the south wing. Here, Captain Remus opened a large door. "Inside," he said.

"Can we have some water, please," I asked, "and bandages?"

Remus sneered. "She'll die soon enough without your help."

We went inside. The door closed and a heavy latch fell into place.

It was dark inside, but not full dark. As my eyes adjusted, I saw we were in a large room partially filled with stacks of building material. There was an outer door in the back wall, but that was even more secure than the door to the hallway. The ceiling was high enough that I couldn't see it clearly in the gloom, but I was pretty sure there wasn't an unlocked trap door in it. The walls, unlike those in the other rooms, were built from rough, local flint—but not rough enough that we could climb them—and the floor was tightly tiled with flat stones. There was no getting over, under or through any of it.

Charlie and I left Kayla sitting near the door and rummaged through the supplies to see if we could find anything useful. There were stacks of building blocks and the terracotta roof tiles, piles of lumber, bags of sand, a few boxes containing bolts of cloth, and a half dozen of the big clay jugs. We took the top off one and found it to be filled with the tar that Cenacus had showed us.

"No water, then?" Charlie said.

I shook my head. "Or food."

We made a mat for Kayla out of the straw used for packing and covered it with cloth. Then we helped her lay down and used more cloth to clean her back as best we could and bind her wounds to staunch the bleeding. Then we waited, Charlie and I sitting silent while Kayla sobbed. Slowly, what little light there was faded, until we were in full dark.

We sat next to her into the night, one on each side, staying close but unable to do anything for her. We took turns sleeping and woke to thin light, stiff and cold from sleeping on the floor. We took advantage of what light there was to make a more thorough search, but there was nothing of use in any of the boxes that we could open.

When Kayla woke, we got more cloth and changed her bandages. It was awkward using such big pieces, so I took one of the building blocks and smashed it against the wall until a sliver of rock fell away.

I dropped the building block and picked up the sliver. "This is flint," I said to Charlie, who was watching. "Remember how Pendragon shaved some off a rock, and how sharp it was?"

We used the flint to cut the fabric, then tore it, making smaller pieces. Which turned out to be a good thing.

The bandages we had put on Kayla the night before were now soaked with clotted blood, and her skin pulled away with them. We were as gentle as we could be, but still it must have hurt. Kayla, however, didn't cry out. When the old bandages were off, we cleaned her wounds. The flesh around them was hot and red and beginning to swell.

"We need some water," I said, "and antiseptic."

"What's antiseptic?" Kayla asked.

"Something to make you feel better," Charlie said.

"Anything would make me feel better right now," she said, "but I don't think they're going to bring it."

We waited, but no one came. The room grew lighter, and hot, as the sun rose high in the sky. The sunny weather had continued unabated, and each day seemed warmer than the last, which made the room uncomfortably hot and stuffy. We used more clean cloth to wipe the sweat from Kayla's face and the blood seeping from her back. The tunic she had been wearing was in tatters, so she took it off and we helped her fashion a new one using the cloth we had found. With her wounds covered she lay on her back, sweating and breathing hard in the heat. I stayed with her, wiping her brow as the light grew dim and the air began to cool. Still, no one came.

Kayla napped, drawing shallow breaths, her forehead hot. She woke as evening approached, sobbing. "My back is burning, and I'm dying of thirst."

"We've got to find something for her," I said.

"Like what?" Charlie asked. "There's nothing here of any real use."

"Stay with her," I said, "I'm going to have another look before it gets too dark to see."

But there was nothing except more building materials. In desperation, I opened all the jugs, just in case one of them held water. When I opened the last one and saw the familiar blackness and caught the sweet scent of sap rising from the opening, I got so mad I kicked the jug over.

It hurt my foot, but the jug tipped and fell, cracking open on the hard ground, letting the tar ooze and spread.

"Way to go, Mitch," Charlie called. "Now the room stinks."

The smell did permeate the room, but it wasn't unpleasant. It smelled of leather and fresh sawdust and, without the overriding scent of burning wood, its familiarity made itself known. I scooped some up in my hand and rolled it between my palms, sniffing as I did.

"We had some of this in school last year," I said.

"Where? In cooking class?" Charlie asked.

"No." I took another sniff. "We were studying the Middle Ages. This stuff has been around a long time. The teacher said some archaeologists think the Neanderthals even knew how to make it."

Charlie stood up and came toward me. "What for? They didn't build houses."

The warmth of my hands made the tar goopy, and I stretched it out, letting it droop between my hands like soft taffy. "It was used for other things," I said, struggling to remember what they were. "They stuck things together with it and made perfume out of it."

"Ugh," Charlie, who was now standing next to me, said.

I held out the glop in my hand. "They even used it as chewing gum."

"No thanks," Charlie said.

"But the other thing they used it for," I said, "was medicine. If I remember right, it's an antiseptic."

We figured there was no harm in trying. We cut more cloth, took off Kayla's bandages and I gently smeared the softened tar on her wounds. When her whole back was covered, we bound her in bandages again and helped her put her tunic on.

She was able to sleep after that, but her fever didn't leave. We'd done all we could, but it wasn't enough. She needed real medicine and proper bandages, and we all needed water.

When full darkness arrived, we settled in for another long night. Then we heard the thump of the latch. The door opened and Fabianus entered, carrying a lantern in one hand and a skin of water in the other. He threw the water to us. The skin landed at my feet with a dull thud. "Does the girl still live?"

"Yes," I said.

Fabianus nodded, his thin lips pulled into a tight grin. "I am master of the amulet, and owner of the cloak, therefore, the gods smile upon me. She should be dead, as should you, but the gods bid me spare you, because you have an important task to perform for me."

"She can't work," I said. "She's hurt."

"She will work," Fabianus said, "and so will you. Drink now, and move. Quickly."

But we didn't drink or move. We gave the water to Kayla and let her drink. When she'd had enough, I carefully poured what was left over her back, wetting her tunic and bandages, trying to cool her wounds. When I was done, there was only enough for me and Charlie to have a single mouthful. It was enough to moisten our parched lips, but that was all. Then the skin was empty.

"Touching," Fabianus said. "You are noble and brave, but foolish. Nothing good will come of your grand gesture. Now come."

Chapter 18

Fabianus led us along the south corridor to another door, double bolted and secured with iron latches. He opened the latches with a bulky key then, looking up and down the corridor, pulled the door open and ushered us inside.

This room was small, no larger than my bedroom back home, lit by four lamps suspended from the ceiling. Much of the floor space was taken up by a strange looking cart, little more than a thick slab of oak held up by wide wooden wheels edged in iron. On the cart was a clay pot about the size of Mom's laundry basket. It was round with a flat bottom that tapered to a smaller opening at the top, which was covered with a lid. Fabianus walked around the cart, running his hand over the surface of the vessel.

"The messenger," he said, staring ahead of him, "the one who interrupted our previous discussion. He brought news of a campaign in the north, which I will be leading, a campaign that will bring much glory to Rome, and to myself, and pave the way for my ascension to Emperor. I leave in ten days." He continued walking, his eyes always staring into the distance, never at us. "As you have ably demonstrated, I cannot trust my slaves, or my soldiers, or my own family, so my wealth—my entire fortune— can be entrusted to no one."

He made another slow circuit around the cart, then thrust his face so suddenly at me that it made me jump. "Do you know the secret of keeping a secret?" he asked, staring hard into my eyes.

"Don't tell anyone," Charlie said.

"Yeah, just keep it a secret," I said. "That's what I'd do."

Fabianus laughed. "Then you're a fool." He climbed onto the cart, lifted the lid of the jug, and peered inside. "The way to keep a secret," he said, "is to keep secret the fact that you have a secret. Now come up here and see my secret."

Charlie and I and Kayla looked at each other, then went to the cart. The bed of the cart was low, but Kayla was unable to climb up without our help. We pulled her up and stood on the opposite side of the pot from Fabianus, clustering close to it so we could look at what was inside. Lit from the lanterns hanging above, the pot appeared to be glowing with fire.

"Gold," Fabianus said. "Gold and silver coins, in a quantity you have never seen before." From a pouch on his belt, he pulled out our bags of coins. He dropped one into the pot—the one with the "M" on it—and held the other for a moment, as if contemplating putting that one in too. After a few moments, he returned it to his pouch. "This is my future, and you are going to guard it for me."

He reached a hand into the pot and caressed the coins.

"I will be absent for many months, so I will send my slaves and guests away. Once I and my soldiers leave, only a trusted few will remain to finish the work on the western wing. But, although I trust them, time could make them curious, and I wouldn't like to think of them stumbling upon this room. The sight of so much wealth can drive a man mad. It must therefore be moved to a place where no one can find it, because no one will know where that is."

He put the lid back on the pot, stepped off the cart and went to another, smaller pot in the corner of the room. Then he came back and slapped a large lump of brown clay onto the lid. "Now seal it. Seal it well."

I poked the clay. It was cold and hard. Charlie picked it up.

"What are we supposed to do with this?" he asked quietly.

Kayla shook her head. "Don't you know?"

She took the clay from Charlie and broke it into three pieces, giving one to me, one to Charlie and taking one herself. "Watch," she said, "and do as I do."

She rolled the clay between her hands and worked it with her fingers. I followed her example and soon the clay became soft. When it was pliable, she told us to roll it into ropes, which she laid around the lid. She then began working it with her fingers, pushing it around the edges of the lid. We helped as best we could, and soon the cover was securely fixed onto the pot, the clay making a nearly airtight seal.

When we were done, Fabianus inspected it and pronounced it sufficient.

He then went to the far wall and slid a crossbar out of its iron fittings, which, it turned out, was keeping the door to the outside secure. He set the wooden bar aside and pushed a set of double doors open, letting in a gush of cool air.

Just outside the door, two donkeys were tethered to a stake.

"Come," he said. "And be quick."

Charlie and I left Kayla on the cart and went to help Fabianus bring the donkeys in.

We helped hitch them to the cart, then secured the pot with stout ropes looped through its side handles. Fabianus put two shovels and a metal bar on the cart and climbed up behind the donkeys.

"Get on the cart," he said, shaking the reins.

The donkey's plodded forward as we climbed back up with Kayla. The cart creaked, the iron-shod wheels turned, and the cart rolled out of the room, out of the villa, and onto the dirt track. We didn't stay on the track, though. Instead, we continued toward the sea.

The night was still, and the creaking of the cart was nearly as loud as the sound of waves rolling onto the shore. I smelled salt in the air, but the sea was hidden in darkness, the sliver of moon casting only a faint glow. Soon, the crunching of rocks became louder than the waves as we rolled over the stony beach. Here, I noticed, we weren't leaving any tracks, and it was then that the cart turned, not toward the city but the other way, out into the darkness.

Fabianus had a lantern with him, but he didn't light it. We travelled along the beach for a while, then turned inland. Once the cart left the stony ground for grassland, the iron wheels made little noise, and the creaking of the cart eased into a quiet rhythm. We were, I thought, as invisible and silent as it was possible to be, a good way to keep us from being attacked by enemies, or seen by anyone in the villa, and I wondered which one Fabianus was more concerned about avoiding.

Chapter 19

When we were far from the villa and could see nothing by blackness around us, Fabianus stopped the cart.

"Girl," Fabianus said. "You will walk in front now."

Wincing with effort, Kayla slid off the cart and walked to the front.

"This was your land," Fabianus said. "It was your playground when you were young. Even in the dark you will recall its secrets. Now lead me to a place where no one goes, where a person can remain safe and unseen."

"She's hurt," I said. "She can't walk that far."

"She will," Fabianus said. "And there will be no tricks, or I will force her to choose which one of your throats I will cut."

We continued on, with Kayla leading us across the dark land toward the darker forest. Fabianus guided the cart, occasionally checking the sky and making marks on a piece of parchment. The ground was firm, and we made good time, but even so Charlie and I eventually had to help the donkeys by pushing the cart as they pulled. We rolled over humps and into dips and around crevasses until we came to the wooded hills. At the base of one of the hills, Kayla stopped.

We were on the top of a low rise, a flat area surrounded by trees and open to the stars. Kayla lowered herself cautiously and sat in the grass. "This is the place," she said. Then she ran her hand over the ground and spoke quietly. "It was a place of peace, in a happier time."

I watched her, amazed at seeing her almost happy, and started toward her to see if she was all right, but Fabianus handed me a shovel. Then he gave the other one to Charlie.

I heard a click and saw a spark. Then another click, and another. Then the lantern caught, and a weak circle of light appeared.

Fabianus held the lantern aloft, giving us maximum light. "Dig," he said. "Here."

Following Fabianus's orders, we removed a circle of sod and began to dig into the rocky soil. It was hard going, and difficult in the dark, and I was soon aching from the exertion. Charlie, too, was slowing down, but we kept going, determined not to show we were tired because we didn't want to give Fabianus an excuse to make Kayla help us. We dug as fast as we could. When it was waist deep, Charlie got into the hole so he could throw the bigger rocks out while I scooped up the gritty soil with the shovel. Fabianus continued to write on the parchment, checking the stars and scanning around him. The sky was just beginning to lighten in the eastern sky when he pronounced the hole to be deep enough. It came up nearly to Charlie's shoulders and I had to help him out.

Fabianus had already unhitched the donkeys, so we maneuverer the cart to the edge of the hole, then tilted it and untied the pot. With our backs and the shovels, we inched the heavy vessel down the sloping cart until, with a deep thud, it slid into the hole.

"Now fill it," Fabianus said.

The filling went quickly. We didn't want to chance breaking the pot, so we shovelled dirt in until it was covered, then tossed the rocks on top, along with the rest of the soil. When that was done, we replaced the sod, tamped it down and scattered the remaining soil over the grass. While we did this, Fabianus hitched up the donkeys and, as the sky grew lighter, we climbed into the cart with the shovels, and Kayla, and started back.

Fabianus didn't need Kayla's help to retrace our steps. He consulted the parchment and steered the donkeys back the way we had come. Charlie and I laid in the cart, hot, dirty, sweaty, and tired. The night had been cooler than the day, but not by much and, strangely, it seemed to be getting hotter, and darker. I looked up, wondering how this could be possible.

"The gods smile upon me again," Fabianus said, also looking into the sky.

Clouds had appeared on the horizon, and were slowly filling the sky, cutting off the light, returning us to darkness and making the air humid and oppressive. It was still dark when we reached the road leading to the villa. Once again, Fabianus took the cart over the rocky beach, leaving no tracks, turning inland only when we arrived at the open doorway. Fabianus had us unhitch the donkeys and hustle the cart inside. Before pulling the doors closed, he looked one way and then the other to be certain no one was about. Then he closed the doors and secured them with the crossbar, sealing us in darkness. The lantern sparked to life, filling the small room with dull, yellow light.

"Follow," Fabianus said.

We left the room. Fabianus locked the door, then led us through the quiet hallway, back to our storeroom prison. He pulled the door open, and we went inside. The door banged shut behind us, leaving us in darkness once again.

"Is that it?" Charlie asked. "Now we just wait here again?"

I heard straw crackle as Kayla laid on the mat. "Don't worry. We won't have long to wait."

That should have been good news, but her voice told otherwise.

"What do you mean?" I asked.

"You heard him," she said. "The way to keep a secret is to keep anyone from knowing you have a secret. And we're the only ones who know."

I felt a familiar chill blooming in my chest. "He's going to kill us, isn't he?"

Kayla didn't answer. She let the silence speak for her.

"But, if he's going to do that," Charlie said, "he had plenty of chances after we buried his gold."

"If he had killed us out there," Kayla said, "someone would have found our bodies. They might wonder why he had taken us out in the night and that might lead them to his money. He needs to kill us here, properly. If he kills us for no reason, people might wonder why. He needs to create a reason"

"Like what?" I asked.

Kayla sighed. "Did you hear the door when Fabianus closed it?"

"Yes."

"Did you hear him lock it?"

I went to the door and gave it a gentle push. The door creaked open, letting in dim light from the hallway.

"He wants us to escape. He probably stationed

guards outside to catch us if we try to leave."

I took a cautious look. The hallway was quiet and seemingly empty. "I can't see any."

"Trust me," Kayla said, "they are there. They will not be far away. If you run, they will kill you."

"And if we stay?" Charlie asked.

"He'll find another excuse. We know about the Talisman. We know where his fortune is buried. There is no way he can let us live."

Charlie and I sat on the floor next to Kayla as an oppressive silence filled the room. None of us spoke. The only sound was the short, panicked gasps of my own breathing.

"There must be something we can do," Charlie said, "we've got bricks, we could block the door, we could create a diversion, we could batter the outside door down—"

Kayla shook her head. "It's hopeless," she said, her voice flat and resigned. "We can't get out, and we have nowhere to run."

Charlie stood up and began pacing. "Then what are we to do?"

Kayla drew a deep breath and closed her eyes. "Do as you will. I'll stay here and wait for whatever finds me first, death, or execution."

Her breathing became shallow. I placed a hand on her forehead. Her brow was hot and moist.

"She's given up," Charlie said. "Help me think of a way to divert the guard's attention. And we can make weapons out of something, anything."

With my hand still on Kayla's forehead, I looked up at him. "We can't leave her."

Charlie thew up his arms in disgust. "So, we just sit here and wait to be executed?"

I tuned him out, thinking hard, watching Kayla, feeling her fever, and fearing she might be right. Every fibre of my being wanted to jump up and rush out the door with Charlie and take our chances. But I forced myself to stay at her side.

"We've no choice," I said. "We made a promise."

"That's insane," Charlie said, his voice rasping as he struggled to keep from shouting. "We're going to die here if we don't do something."

"We won't," I said, not feeling at all confident in my words, "there were other promises made."

I leaned down, putting my lips close to Kayla's ear.

"You must get up," I whispered. "I watched as you looked into the Talisman. You have a stalwart heart; what it showed you was true, and you know this in your soul. You are to be the mother of kings. You are not meant to die here. You've gotta help us find a way out."

Kayla moaned and shook her head.

I sat up, out of ideas, out of hope, and running out of time.

"At least let me dress your wounds," I said. "There's more of that Birch-Tar."

I started to get up, but Kayla grabbed my arm. She was still strong despite her fever.

"No," she said.

I tried to pull away from her. "I know it won't matter, but I can't do nothing, I promised—"

"Not my back," she said, struggling to sit up. "The tar. I have an idea. But you must hurry."

Chapter 20

Following Kayla's instructions, we gathered more cloth and a pile of the straw. I used a building stone to bash the wall and break off a few hunks of flint. Then she had us smear the cloth with the birch-bark tar and wrap strips of tar-soaked cloth around the ends of some short poles we found.

Meanwhile, Kayla teased threads from a strip of cloth to make a small, fluffy ball. She then struck the stones together, making sparks fly into the threads. One of the sparks landed in the threads and began to glow. She blew on it but, after glowing bright for a few seconds, it went out. She struck the stones again and again and another spark began to burn. This one, too, went out as she tried to nurse it into a flame. A third time the threads began to glow. She breathed gently into the ember, and it grew. Then a tiny flame erupted. "Quick, the torches."

Charlie held a small piece of pitch-soaked cloth over the tiny flame, and it soon caught, and the fire spread rapidly.

"What the …" Charlie said, dropping the cloth. It laid on the stone floor, burning away.

"Add more cloth," Kayla said, "a little at a time, and light the torches."

We held the poles over the fire, setting them alight.

"Now smear some tar on the floor, and on the door.

Both sides."

I pulled the door closed so anyone in the hallway wouldn't be alerted by the light. Then I took Charlie's torch while he ran and brought a section of the broken jug—filled with tar—back. We used a cloth to spread it over the floor, then smeared the inside of the door.

"Is anyone out there?" Charlie asked.

I pushed the door open a crack and peered through. "The coast looks clear," I said.

Charlie slipped outside and smeared the outer surface of the door.

"Now light the floor," Kayla said, "and both sides of the door. Then run. I'll stay and detain them as long as I can."

"No, you won't," I said, handing my torch to Charlie. I grabbed her by the arms and lifted her, struggling, to her feet. "You're coming with us."

I pulled her toward the door as Charlie lit the tar on the floor. The tar was cold, so it didn't light easily, but once it started, it burned quickly. I pulled Kayla through the open door.

"Light the door, Charlie," I whispered, "and run."

We ran down the hall as fast as we could, pulling Kayla with us. I headed toward the west wing, hoping we could get out that way. Seconds later, someone shouted, "Fire."

"Hide," Kayla said, "behind the columns."

We ran into the shadows and crouched on the floor. I tried to calm my breathing, so I didn't give our hiding place away, but I needn't have worried.

More voices called out. "Fire!" Feet pounded down the hallway. "The storeroom's on fire."

People raced past us toward the burning storeroom, which was already lighting up the hall.

134

"Quickly! Fire! Help!"

More people ran past. Then soldiers, and soon a crowd had gathered. The soldiers shouted orders, people carrying buckets of water began to douse the flaming door, several soldiers rushed inside, heedless of the smoke billowing from the opening.

"Where are they?" came a shout. "Find them."

"Now," Kayla said. "Move."

We kept to the shadows, moving up the hall.

"We need to get to the west wing," I said. But then I heard more pounding feet. Another squad of soldiers were coming our way. From within the growing crowd, I heard Captain Remus's voice, rising above the pandemonium. "Do not let them escape."

"This way," Kayla said.

She led us down a corridor and through an open door.

"Upstairs, quickly."

It was one of the wooden stairways up to the slave quarters.

"Quiet," she said. "We don't want to draw attention."

The upstairs hallway was nearly pitch black, but Kayla felt her way along with practiced ease. She pulled a door open, and we all ducked inside.

"This is my room," she said.

"Don't you think they'll search this?" Charlie asked. "They're probably on their way right now."

"Of course they are," she said. "That's why we're not staying."

There was a small window in the room, a grey rectangle in the dimness. Kayla went to it and began pulling on the bottom sill. "Help me."

Charlie and I joined her. The concrete along the

base of the window began to crumble.

"I've been pouring water on it every day," she said. "It weakens it. They don't use the best materials for the slave's rooms."

Some of the concrete broke away, then a bit more. We pulled harder. A block came loose and thudded to the floor.

Kayla looked through the widened hole. "Can you fit through that?"

"Can you?" I asked. "You first. We don't know where we are."

I also didn't trust her to follow us. Thankfully, she didn't object, she wriggled her head and shoulders through the opening and squirmed through. It must have been unbearably painful for her back, but she didn't make a sound. As soon as she was through, Charlie went, then I followed.

The window opened onto the roof of a long porch. It was pitched, but not steeply. The villa's roof overhung the wall of the slave quarters, but we couldn't reach it to climb up.

"We can jump off here and get a way," I said.

Kayla shook her head. "This is in internal roof. You'll land in one of the gardens and be trapped. Follow me."

We ran along the top of the porch and scrambled onto another that branched off at a right angle. Sunrise was an hour or two away, but clouds covered the sky, keeping the light dim. Still, it was bright enough that anyone looking up would certainly see us. And anyone out for an early stroll on the porch would clearly hear us thumping overhead. There wasn't anything to be done about that, though, except run faster.

By the time we got to the next corner, Charlie and I

were tired, but Kayla was exhausted. Whatever reserves she had been drawing on were nearly empty. We climbed onto the next roof and ran, somewhat slower, to the construction area. The roof of the porch was still below the roof of the main building, making it impossible to climb over to the outside, but where the new pool was being installed, there was a peaked roof that came down to the level of the porch. We climbed onto that and scrambled over the roof to the other side. There were men already on site, laying roof tiles and working on the outdoor pool, so we slipped back to the other side and moved on. When we judged we had gone far enough, we climbed over again, slid down the tiles to the edge of the roof, and then dropped onto the porch below.

The porch roof was narrow, so Charlie and I jumped first, so we could catch Kayla and keep her from sliding off. We moved to the edge. The ground looked a long way down.

"Do you think you can make it?" I asked Kayla.

"There they are," someone shouted.

"Yes," she said, and jumped.

I jumped after her, with Charlie right behind. I landed hard and felt a twinge in my side. Charlie hit the ground with a thud. Kayla was lying on the grass in front of me.

"Run," I said, grabbing her by an arm.

Charlie helped me get her to her feet. Her head lolled as she tried to focus. "North," she said. "The forest."

We set off, holding Kayla between us, trotting over the grassy fields toward the looming trees. Until we made the cover of the forest, we were painfully exposed. I ran on, mindful of Kayla lolling ever more loosely between us.

There was still a hundred yards to go when I heard shouting behind us. I didn't turn or pause; I knew the voices. It was Captain Remus and his lieutenants Cato and Gaius. We ran harder, trying not to give in to exhaustion. Slowly, the trees came closer, but behind us the voices sounded louder.

When at last we entered the forest, I thought we were home free, but instead, things got worse. The thick trees blotted out the weak light and we had to pick our way through the gloom. And we didn't dare fall. If we did, we would never get up. Behind us, the soldiers blundered into the woods, slashing and shouting and closing the small gap between us with sickening speed. I struggled to increase my pace, but it was no use. They would be on us in seconds.

Then a hand grabbed me from behind.

I tried to call out, but another hand covered my mouth. In the confusion, I saw Charlie and Kayla also being pulled into the bushes. In a matter of moments, I was sitting on the ground, my arms pinned, and my mouth clamped shut. Beside me, Charlie—also held and silenced by an unseen captor—looked at me with wide eyes. Kayla was there too, but her mouth was not covered; she lay limp against her captor, her head lying to one side. Other dark figures approached, making not a sound. They didn't look at Charlie or me but watched the clearing they had snatched us from. A second later, the soldiers—swords and torches held high—charged in.

Captain Remus held up a hand and they stopped, listening, and looking around them.

"They've disappeared," Cato said.

"They couldn't have just vanished—" Gaius began.

"There are those who can," Remus said, cutting him off. "And if these fugitives have their help, we will not find them." He scanned the bushes, looking directly at us, but not seeing. In my side vision, I saw a dark figure raise a bow and draw back an arrow.

"We can't go back without them," Gaius said. "Fabianus will have our heads."

"You can go on," Captain Remus said, "but remember, a Celt can come up behind you and slit your throat before you hear him coming. That girl is a Celt, and those boys have Celt blood. You go, I'll return to Fabianus and tell him of your demise."

"And Fabianus will see you dead."

Remus stepped backward and sheathed his sword. "Listen to me," he said. "We chased the fugitives into the sea, and the current washed their bodies away." He held out a hand to his men and the three of them clasped hands. "Stay true to that story, and each other, and we just may keep our lives."

They nodded to one another, dropped their hands, and started back the way they had come. The dark archer lowered his bow and the forest returned to silence.

Chapter 21

The men who took us were lean and strong. They wore sleeveless tunics, short enough to pass as shirts, long pants held up with twine, and soft shoes that looked like moccasins. Their clothing was all green or brown and their skin was weathered and dark and featured tattoos of complex, interwoven designs. Their heads were shaved, though a bristle of red hair sprouted from a few of them. There were five in all, one holding each of us, the archer and another carrying what looked like a short axe.

When the soldiers left, the one with the axe stood up. He was tall and thin but with bulging muscles. He looked around, then lowered himself and moved silently toward me. He put his face near mine and held a finger to his lips. I nodded and the hand left my mouth. I gulped in a lungful of air but said nothing.

Axeman went to Charlie and did the same thing. He nodded to the man cradling Kayla, limp in his arms, and he ran into the woods, carrying her like a baby. Then he looked at Charlie and me and indicated we should follow.

We ran into the forest, them silently, and us not so silently. I was so tired I began to stumble and the man who had held me now grabbed my arm impatiently and pulled me along. Charlie, too, was falling behind, and was being dragged by the archer and another man.

Axeman stayed in front, leading us.

Half an hour later, we came to a small clearing where several crude shelters made of branches and animal hides were clustered around a fire. To one side, about ten horses were tied among the trees.

As our group entered the clearing, half a dozen men emerged from the huts. Most, like the men with us, were tall and muscular, wearing loose pants, moccasins and sleeveless shirts that showed off the tattoos swirling down their arms. These men carried swords, axes, knives, and round metal shields intricately inlaid with designs matching their tattoos.

We were dragged to the edge of the fire and released, and I wondered—not for the first time—if we had been rescued or taken captive again. There was no sign of Kayla, or the man who had run off with her. I wanted to ask but I wasn't sure if I was allowed to speak yet, and the man who emerged from one of the huts and came our way didn't seem in the mood for conversation.

He was tall and powerfully built but, unlike the others, he had shoulder-length hair and a short beard the colour of rust speckled with white. He wore a longer shirt and leather boots that came to his calves. His eyes were a deep blue and he fixed them on us with undisguised contempt. I didn't want to appear weak in front of him, but I was beyond exhausted, and both Charlie and I were dirty and dishevelled and hardly impressive looking. He stood between us and the fire, making me suddenly cold, and I struggled not to shiver.

"Were they where Meryn said they'd be?"

"Yes, Talan," the man carrying the axe said.

"Romans?"

"Three pursuers."

"Did you kill them?"

There was a short silence. "No," the man said.

Talan glared at him. "Why not?"

"It might have brought others."

"Then you could have killed them too."

Axeman, tall and powerful as he was, shuffled nervously under Talan's gaze.

"And these puny children were the only ones there?" Talan asked. "Were there no others?"

"There was a third, a slave girl. She is with the Healer."

"Wounded?"

"Whipped, and fever has entered her wounds."

"Then she is of no concern," Talan said, turning his gaze back to me and Charlie. "But you, pathetic vagabonds. Meryn would have me believe you are the ones of whom the prophecy speaks. I would kill you both now and save myself the trouble of bringing you to him if I didn't wish to see the look on the old mystic's face when I present you to him." To the men standing with us, he said, "Prepare to travel. We leave immediately."

The men dismantled the huts, returning the branches to the forest and packing the skins. The fire was doused, and the ashes scattered. Soon, the clearing looked as if no one had been there.

Horses were led to us. They had strange looking saddles, but we were told to mount them, so I struggled up onto mine and tried to look confident sitting up on its back. The others mounted, also, and the small group, with Talan in the lead, headed out of the clearing and into the forest. We followed, riding in single file, with the archer and Axeman behind us.

We moved along a narrow path for a while, then

came to a wider track, then a dirt road and, finally, a paved thoroughfare where the horses, alarmingly, broke into a gallop.

I held on with my last bit of strength and wondered if we were on one of the roads the Romans had built and, if so, how we were going to avoid running into them. This question was answered later in the morning when, at a signal from Talan, the men and horses scattered into the woodlands beside the road. Axeman and the archer led our horses deep into the forest, and motioned for us to keep silent.

I waited. Charlie looked at me, a puzzled expression on his face. I shrugged and waited some more. Then came the sound of tramping feet, a distant thump, thump, thump that grew louder and larger with each thud. Then, through the branches and leaves, I saw a column of Roman soldiers, led by four men on horseback, march past. They moved fast, in perfect step, and there had to be hundreds of them. When they passed and the tramping of their feet faded, we waited some more, then Talan signalled to us, and we went back to the road.

This went on for hours and I occasionally found myself falling asleep with the horse galloping under me, only to be jolted awake as I began to slip. Finally, when the sun was high overhead, Talan led the group off the road and deep into the forest. There, the men ate and drank while Charlie and I dropped, exhausted, to the forest floor and fell promptly to sleep.

We were awakened at dusk and, again, offered food and drink. This time, we accepted, gulping the cool water, and wolfing down the cold meat and cheese. And, like before, when we left the temporary campsite, no trace of our passing was left behind. To my surprise, we didn't return to the road, but instead rode deeper into the forest.

Talan led us at a fast pace and, even though we weren't moving at the breakneck speed we had been travelling when we were on the road, we struggled to keep up. It wasn't dark yet, but the shadows were long and deep, and I remained perpetually terrified of running headlong into a tree, which served to keep me awake and alert.

The moon was just over half full and, where the trees were sparse, it cast just enough light for us to see shapes among the shadows. Talan, however, seemed to have no need of light, for our pace never wavered, even when we travelled through the densest of woods.

We travelled until the sky grew light and the sun rose, then we stopped and made another camp. Although the knowledge of how to ride a horse remained with me from our time with Pendragon, the callouses had not, and I climbed off the horse on shaky legs and slumped to the ground. I was, once again, too tired to think about eating, so I crawled—along with Charlie, who seemed to feel the same as I did—to a grassy spot where we flopped flat on our stomachs, because our backsides felt as if they were on fire, and went to sleep.

Hours later we were awakened and travelled on. The afternoon was agony, even with the extra blanket the archer had kindly provided for me when he saw me limping. With the benefit of daylight, we rode faster, sometimes in forests, sometimes on broad, grassy plains, and other times—at a full gallop—along straight, even roads.

As the sun dropped low in the western sky, we approached a strange looking hill. It was broad and flat on the top, its massive base completely encircled with a steep ring of earth. In the centre of the flat top sat another ring. When we drew closer, we saw people and horses and carts and realized the hill was much larger than it first seemed.

The people, dressed in long shirts and loose trousers, or simple dresses of different colours, were coming and going from a single point at the base of the hill, where it met a road. Since the day was ending, most of the people were returning, carrying bundles, or driving carts filled with goods. Our group of riders joined the road and the people made way for us, staring with awe at the muscular, tattooed warriors.

The road that led into the hill rose up the side of the massive earth-ring and through a cutting near the top. The edges of the cutting were twice the height of Talan on his horse, and the ditch on the far side of the cutting was twice as deep. We crossed the ditch over a wooden bridge and entered the huge, flat area inside the ring and continued on the path toward the second hill.

The second hill was surrounded by a deep trench, like a moat without water, and beyond that, another, smaller ring of earth. We crossed the trench on a narrow bridge that angled steeply up the side of the ring, over the top, and sharply down the other side. Then, suddenly, we were in a village.

The smells of wood smoke, cooking meat, animal excrement and mud hit me all at once. Cows, sheep, and pigs wandered the muddy lanes between the thatched cottages, which appeared to be randomly scattered throughout the centre circle. Throngs of people continued to arrive, passing by us to enter the village, heedless of the mud and livestock.

Talan halted by the edge of the village, bringing our

horses even with his, and holding the reins so we didn't wander off, while the rest of the band gathered behind us. I wanted badly to dismount, but Talan remained still, as if he was waiting for something.

Then, moving against the throngs entering the village came a figure dressed in a long white robe, his face obscured by a hood. The figure moved slowly, gliding over the mud and muck, and stopped in front of us. The shadow beneath the hood turned toward Talan.

"Here is your warrior, and your wise man," Talan said, throwing the reins of our horses into the mud. "Are these the ones you sent me for? The ones who are to return what was taken? These vagabond children? The only reason I don't kill you where you stand is that I wish you to witness the deaths of these Roman whelps first."

The figure stood, silent. Talan spat into the mud at the figure's feet.

"Find your courage," he said sounding disgusted. "Admit to me, here, in front of these witnesses, that the prophecy is a myth, and you are a fraud, and meet your death like a man."

Still, the figure said nothing, but moved silently to stand in front of our horses. There, he pulled back his hood, revealing a head of long grey hair, a flowing beard that nearly obscured his mouth, and piercing eyes of icy blue. His eyebrows were bushy and as grey as his hair and beard, except for the right one, where a scar—beginning in the centre of his cheek and cutting around the corner of his eye like a question mark— crossed through it. There the hairs were snowy white.

I stared down at him, unable to speak. Charlie, too, kept silent. Then the man smiled and said, "Hell-o,

Mitch. Hell-o, Charlie. I am Meryn, and I have been expecting you."

Chapter 22

"It was our names that saved us," I said, scooping up another mouthful of cold stew.

It was the following day, around noon, I judged, even though there was no sun to go by. The sky remained covered by low, grey clouds, keeping the still air moist and oppressively hot. We had awakened in the hut Meryn had led us to the night before and found it empty, except for two bowls of a thin vegetable stew. We had no idea if it was meant for us, but we were hungry, so we ate it.

Talan had wanted to execute us on the spot when we had arrived at the village, which we now knew was called Sarum, and the arrival of the Druid had only stiffened his resolve. That is, until I recognized him, and he called us by name. Then Talan's contempt turned to disappointment, and rage. He called Meryn a charlatan, and ordered his men to take him prisoner, but Meryn had held up his hand to stay them and surprisingly, they had obeyed. This angered Talan even more, but Meryn ignored him. He helped us down from the horses and led us away, into the small village, down its narrow, muddy streets, to a small, stone hut.

There, we found beds already prepared for us and, with a hundred questions in my mind, I laid down next to Charlie and fell asleep. When we woke, we found no one else in the small hut, and a peek through the single, tiny window—which revealed a narrow, muddy street lined with other stone buildings, and crowded with people going about whatever business people in Roman Britain got up to during the day—convinced us to stay

"How do you figure that?" Charlie asked through a mouthful of stew.

"I'm not sure," I said, "all I know is Talan was ready to kill us, but when the Druid called us by name, it deflated him. I guess he was counting on the Druid, Meryn, to say we weren't the ones he was looking for."

"Are we, though?"

I stirred the wooden spoon around in the congealing stew. "I'm not sure. But I do wonder how he knew our names."

"Duh," Charlie said, "he's met us before."

I shook my head. "He hasn't though. He won't meet us for another couple of centuries. That was what he meant when he told you and me and Pendragon that night in the forest about it being the second time he had seen us, but only the first time we had seen him."

"That's crazy."

"You doubt what you know you have seen," came a voice. The hut's interior suddenly lit up as the door opened and Meryn stepped inside. "Yet there are men who become convinced by things they think they see. You have an admirably questioning mind, young Charlie."

Before the light was cut off by the closing of the door, I saw the hut contained only a few pieces of crude furniture, and a small fire pit near the far wall. There was no fire in it, yet the air in the room remained hot and smoky. Meryn was no longer dressed in the white robe, and instead wore a tan tunic and loose pants. His hair and beard were grey but there was a little brown mixed in, making him appear younger than the last time we'd seen him, which, I supposed, he was.

"How did you know our names?" Charlie asked as Meryn closed the door and sat at the low table with us. "Mitch says you've never met us before."

"Indeed, I have not," the Druid said.

"Yet you know who we are," I said, "and we—who have met you before—didn't know your name."

Meryn rubbed his chin through his thick beard. "That is a conundrum."

"Well, we didn't know your name because you never told us," I said, "and you called us by name the first time we met you because you told us you had met us before."

"And here I am meeting you for the first time, and you are meeting me for the second."

"That's right."

"And you are certain you are not mistaken."

I shook my head. "No," I said, "it was definitely you." I traced the route of his scar on my face.

Meryn touched his own scar. "When was this first meeting?"

I thought it over, trying to recall the little I knew of the Arthurian legend and the Romans. "About two hundred years from now."

Meryn nodded slowly and remained quiet for several minutes.

"Then what the elders have foreseen is true," he said at last. "And if that is so, a long journey awaits me."

"But it was just a year ago we met," Charlie said, "maybe it will just be another year until you meet us again."

Meryn shook his head. "We are very different, you and I," he said. "Our quest is the same, but our paths are wide apart."

I took another taste of stew, which was surprisingly good, despite being cold. "I don't get you."

Meryn went silent again, this time for so long I wondered if he had fallen asleep.

"Think of the night sky," he said. "The stars, spread across the heavens, filling the night with specks of light, always there, moving with the seasons, but always returning to the same place. They are the eternal lights. But among them, there are wanderers, lights that travel their own path, moving among the stars, appearing here, then there."

He sighed then and seemed troubled. "You are wanderers," he said. "And I am the stars."

I waited for him to say something else. When he didn't, I asked what had happened to Kayla. That only seemed to make him more thoughtful.

"The girl you had with you is now with the gods," he said. "For now, you must not concern yourself with her."

The news stung me. I dropped my spoon and pushed the bowl away. Was she dead? Had we failed her? After all the risks we had taken, all the hardships we had overcome. It didn't seem fair. And Ameena, what could I tell her?

"We made a promise—"

Meryn cut me off. "And you kept that promise as well as you could. But there are others who need saving. Just as you played a role with the girl, you must now play a role with Talan."

"Talan," Charlie said. "I thought we were done with him."

Meryn shook his head slowly. "You remain his prisoners, and he continues to long for your blood. I am allowed to look after you for now, but a decision must soon be made as to whether Talan will have his way, or you are allowed to fulfil your destiny."

"Decision?" I asked. "Destiny?"

Charlie folded his arms across his chest. "What is it with Talan? Why are we his prisoners? What does he have against us? We've never done anything to him."

Meryn looked at Charlie and, leaning forward, pointed to his scar. "The Romans gave me this," he said. "But, in time, the blood stopped flowing, the wound healed, I forgot the pain." Sighing, he leaned back. "Talan's wounds, I fear, run deeper."

"But what's that got to do with us?"

Meryn placed his elbows on the low table and rested his bearded chin on his fists. "Talan is a brave warrior and worthy chief. He is well-versed in the art of war and is a formidable ally in our quest to defeat the Romans. But he has suffered much at their hands, and he has allowed his grief to fester and turn bitter. He fights now, not with justice in his heart, but a desire for revenge, and this has tainted his soul. His fury has blinded him to the prophecy, causing him to ignore what he knows to be true, urging him—against his nature—to see you, not as the answer, but as an opportunity to make a futile stab at his enemies. He thinks killing you will hurt the Romans. He refuses to see that you are the key to defeating them. His rage has turned him from a friend to an enemy."

Charlie's brow furrowed. "So …?"

"So, the first thing we must do is save him from himself."

"How?" I asked.

Meryn looked at me. "Trust," he said, "and have courage."

"I don't like the sound of that," Charlie said.

I held my head in my hands, afraid all the questions I had would make it explode. "We can't defeat the Romans. Neither can Talan. All of us put together can't defeat them. So why fight them? And even if you could beat them ... the farm, that palace, the city, the roads ... they are so ... you could learn things from them."

Meryn stood and began pacing in a tight circle, which was all the small room allowed.

"The Romans are a clever people," he said, looking straight ahead as he spoke, "and I do not deny their world holds many advantages over ours, but while their advances show cunning and perception, they lack understanding. The Land, for them, is not something to live in harmony with, it is there only to conquer, to subdue, to bend to their will.

"They do not respect the Land, they defile it, disrespect it, and fail to understand it is a living, breathing being in its own right. The Land cares for us, but only so long as we care for the Land. The Romans do not; they will continue to despoil, and if they continue to disinherit people from the Land, there will come a time when the Land itself will be threatened with destruction; the groves, the streams, the very sky will wither and fade and, without them, we will all die."

He stopped speaking then, but continued to pace, faster, with his head lowered, staring at the ground.

"Is that why you fight them?" I asked. "Because they disrespect the Land?"

Meryn stopped pacing and chuckled. Then he looked at me and smiled. "No," he said. "We fight them because they mean to kill us all. That they

153

disrespect the Land, that is why they will fail."

He began pacing again, more slowly this time. "The Land will reject them. Of that, I am certain. The time of the Romans is ending. Or it should be, except now they possess the beating heart of the Land, and this has upset the balance."

"You're talking about the Talisman," Charlie said.

Meryn nodded. "Without it, the Land mourns and its powers fades, and we will lose the power we draw from the living Land, and the Romans—or someone like them—will continue to build villas and roads and seek to enslave the Land and strip it of its majesty. The Land will always resist, but so long as the Romans hold the Talisman, this land they call Britannia, will never be free of them."

"But there's nothing we can do about that," I said.

Meryn stopped and looked at us. "You alone know where the Talisman is; you alone are able to retrieve it. You are the ones chosen to return that which has been taken, because you have been touched by the Talisman."

Charlie sat back and folded his arms across his chest again. "Yeah, okay, we do know where the Talisman is, so why don't we tell you and you can go get it?"

Meryn shook his head, the hint of a smile visible through his moustache and beard. "Would that it were so simple. True, the Celts are cunning and skilled warriors, but the Romans are many and strong. Without intimate knowledge of the palace, they could never hope to elude the guards and, once discovered, they would be killed."

Neither Charlie nor I said anything; we both knew it was true.

"You know the palace," Meryn said. "You know

154

how to get in, how to get out, and where to find what you are looking for."

"But that doesn't mean we want to go back," I said.

Meryn's smile widened. "I am sure you don't. Only a fool would wish to return to such a place. Talan wants to go, but only to satisfy his rage in slaughter. His warriors want to go, but only so they may be sung about in poems around our campfires. Their efforts would end in failure. But you, who do not wish to go, will go, because you must."

I was momentarily puzzled. I stared down at the tabletop, and then it came to me. "Our cloak," I said. "We have to go back. It's the only way can get our cloak."

I sat in stunned silence. Meryn remained still, waiting while Charlie and I grappled with the inevitable.

"If we have to go back," Charlie said, "we need to go soon."

Now that the decision had been made, a sudden urgency gripped me, and I jumped to my feet. "We need to go now," I said. "There's not much time. Fabianus is leaving; he'll take our cloak, and the Talisman, with him."

Meryn came to me and put a hand on my shoulder. "What you say is true, but the time is not yet right."

"What do you mean by that?" Charlie asked, also getting to his feet. "Mitch is right; we have to go. Now."

Meryn turned away and went to a wooden chest on the other side of the room. "If you try to leave now the warriors will kill you before you reach the gates." He pulled a white robe from the chest and put it on. "Do not forget your station; you are captives, and the village elders are meeting now to decide your fate." He cinched his robe, picked up a staff that was leaning against the wall and turned to face us. The white robe, weathered and stained with mud, hung to his feet, its long sleeves covering all but the tips of his fingers. Standing in silence, with the staff clutched in his hand and his face shrouded in shadow by the hood, Meryn looked suddenly sinister.

Charlie gaped at Meryn, his mouth open, and I noticed I was doing the same. Then Meryn laughed.

"People expect to see a Druid in a robe and holding a staff," he said, spreading his arms. "It adds a bit of gravitas, don't you think?"

Charlie turned to me, a bewildered look on his face.

"Come," Meryn said. "It is time."

I felt my stomach lurch. "Time for what?"

"Time to save Talan."

We left the hut, following Meryn into the muggy afternoon, through the strangely empty streets, to a hard-trodden track leading out of the settlement. Beyond the edge of the village, near the inner trench, a crowd of people clustered around a solitary figure. The man wore a gold helmet, and a jewelled sword hung from his belt. He was dressed in a long tunic and a scarlet cape, and stood with his back to us, facing a line of five other men. Three of the men were dressed in tunics and capes, the other two in grey robes, and each one looked stone-faced and sombre.

Meryn steered us toward the babbling throng. As we drew near, the voices of the crowd rose, and the solitary figure turned to face us. It was Talan, standing with one fisted hand resting on his hip, the other on the hilt of his sword. Of all the people in the gathering, he was the only one smiling, but his smile did not convey welcome; it was more like the leer of a wolf.

I grabbed Charlie by an arm and we both stopped. "What's going on?" I asked.

"Your trial," Meryn said, not looking our way. "This is where your fate, and the fate of the Land, will be decided."

Chapter 23

I stood, frozen to the spot, holding Charlie's arm. "Trial? But we haven't done anything wrong."

"Yeah," Charlie said, "we're not criminals."

"Your actions are not at issue," Meryn said. "It is who you are that the Council will decide."

I looked up at Meryn, who was watching Talan. "And who are we?"

"You are the best hope Talan, his people, and the Land have. But Talan must be convinced of that."

"We're not even convinced of that," I said. "Can't you just let us go so we can try to get our cloak back?"

Meryn shook his head. "Do not forget who holds the power here. The Council may run the village, but I am merely a lone figure without allies, and Talan, though a beneficiary of Sarum's hospitality, has his warriors with him. This, despite the laws of the land, gives him the power. It took much convincing before he agreed to this trial. If I, and the Council, had not been able to persuade him, you would already be in his hands. This trial is your best and only hope."

He urged us forward. I took a step. Then another.

"You'll get us off, then?" Charlie asked.

My insides grew cold as the Druid kept silent. Then, after a few more steps, he said, "Talan wants your blood. The Council finding against him will not shift that desire, and I fear what he cannot get by the law he may decide to take by force."

As we drew closer, the crowd began to murmur. The sound grew louder the closer we came, and I had to raise my voice so Meryn could hear me. "What can we do?"

"Trust," Meryn said, "and have courage."

The crowd, which had allowed a wide path, now closed around us, locking us in with the Council and Talan, who watched us with wolf-like eyes as we approached. Hoots and jeers erupted as we entered the circle. I heard cries of, "Romans," and calls for blood, which made my own feel like ice. When we drew even with Talan, he turned to face the Council, along with us and Meryn. The five men stood silent, looking from Talan to Meryn with neutral expressions. At a signal from one of the Councillors, a man waiting nearby came toward us holding shackles. Meryn put a hand up and shook his hooded head. The man looked at the Council, who all gave barely perceptible nods, and the man retreated, taking the shackles with him. The crowd expressed their displeasure by shouting louder. Then one of the Councillors, dressed in a grey robe, stepped forward carrying a stone, black as the Talisman but shaped like a ball. The man held the ebony sphere aloft, then placed it in Meryn's outstretched hand. Almost immediately the crowd grew quiet, and an eerie silence descended.

Above us the slate sky stretched, merging with the earthen walls of the inner defences, making it appear as if the small village, and the gathering of silent people, were the whole of the world. The air was stifling and still; not a leaf fluttered, not a blade of grass wavered. Then a voice broke the spell.

"Meryn, chief of the Druids, keeper of the

mysteries, custodian of truths," the councillor at the end of the line, who I assumed must be the head councillor because he was dressed in an ornate tunic and cape and had a gold chain around his neck, said, his voice booming in the still, silent air, "what say you about these boys?"

Meryn faced them, his fingers curled around the black stone. He looked from them to me, then Charlie, and then turned to the crowd standing behind us. "Respected elders and priests of Sarum," he said, "I speak only the truth: seven years before the Talisman was taken, the gods favoured a Druid princess with a vision of what was to come. The prophecy revealed that travellers from a land we know nothing of would come—a warrior and a wise man—to return that which was taken. Seven years after the prophecy, our villages were destroyed, and the Talisman stolen."

Talan made a noise, a small sound that would have gone unnoticed if it hadn't been for the unearthly silence. I looked and saw his face contort into a mixture of grief and rage, and again he emitted the sound, like a wounded animal, ready to strike at its attacker. Meryn ignored him.

"And now," he continued, "seven years since that day, these boys have arrived to fulfil the prophecy. They are the Guardians of the Talisman. It is they who will return it to its rightful owners. That is the truth; I have nothing more to say."

The man in the grey robe came forward again and took the stone from Meryn's hand. As soon as he did, the crowd erupted, hooting and jeering, until Talan accepted the stone and silence returned.

Talan nodded toward the five councillors, then turned slowly to scan the faces in the crowd, from one end to the other. I followed his gaze and saw Talan's warriors among the villagers, spaced throughout the crowd. Then Talan's voice cut through the still air. "My friends," he said, "my brothers. You have shown kindness and great bravery in providing sanctuary for us. We appreciate your kindness, but we respect your bravery even more."

He turned and looked at Meryn. "Meryn may be chief of the Druids, but I am chief of the Celts. These boys are my prisoners, and I will not leave this assembly without them. In the seven years that the Druids have been scanning the heavens, looking for a sign, I and my warriors have been fighting the Romans, driving them from your homes, your villages, your land. In those years, have the mystics conjured a way to return the Talisman? Have they brought our captives back? Have they brought the Land any closer to redemption?"

Talan raised his fist with the black stone clutched in it and the crowd roared, "No."

I looked around. Talan's warriors were leading the chants, stirring those around them to echo their emotions. Soon, silence returned, and Talan continued.

"A warrior," he said, looking at Charlie, then he looked directly at me, "and a wise man. This is what the mystic would have us believe, that the gods sent these children to help us."

The crowd began to jeer again; Talan raised his hand to silence them. "But I would not say our Druid chief is wrong; perhaps he is right, but perhaps his vision is clouded from looking too closely. Perhaps he is too willing to believe because he has waited so long. I will tell you truth about these children: they were captured trying to escape from Fabianus, the very

Roman who pillaged us, whose legions killed your families."

His voice faltered. Then he drew a breath and continued. "The Druids believe they are the answer to the prophecy. You have only to look at them to know this is not true. They are nothing but Roman slaves, yet they may still serve the prophecy. Fabianus desires their return. We can stab at him by denying him that, and if they be gifts from the gods, then I say we sacrifice them. Only then will the gods favour us with cunning, strength, and bravery. Their spilled blood will weaken the enemy; their beating hearts will give us power. We, not a pair of slave children, will take back the Talisman."

The crowd erupted again, led by Talan's warriors, cheering and shouting and, from the cacophony, came a growing chant of "sacrifice them, sacrifice them." Though sweating in the stifling air, I found myself shivering. Talan raised his arms and gradually brought the crowd under control. "Esteemed elders," he said, when silence returned, "respected priests, give your judgment: do these captives remain mine, or do they go with the Druid? Are we going to allow children to return that which has been taken, or do we spill their blood and take it ourselves?"

The crowd shouted again, calling for war, calling for blood, calling for sacrifice. Talan made no move to quell them and, as the chants grew louder, the Councillors began to shuffle nervously. Slowly, the crowd inched forward, their fists raised, pumping the air. The deafening noise drowned out calls for order from the Councillors. The crowd pressed closer, their faces merging into a contorted mask of mindless rage.

Then Meryn raised his arms and looked to the sky,

his staff pointing toward the heavens. Seconds later, a flash of white light and a crack of thunder broke the spell. Silence returned, the crowd shrank back, and heavy rain fell from the leaden sky. Meryn stepped up to Talan, who was looking around stunned, and plucked the stone from his fist. Then he stepped away, back to where we were standing, and faced the Councillors.

"My friends," he said, his voice booming over the rain. "Your decision is unnecessary. I will spare you from the folly of consigning your peaceful lives to ruin, and I would keep your priests from becoming party to this dark deed, one which our forefathers, in their wisdom, turned away from long ago. No, the decision is not yours to make." He paused and turned to look at the crowd. "For you will not make it with your heart or your head, but out of fear, and that will diminish you."

He turned back to the Council, holding the black ball aloft, even though the only sound was the rain. "I will make the decision: the boys are Talan's prisoners and so they will remain. What say you, Talan? Do you still wish to sacrifice them?"

My stomach dropped and Charlie gripped my arm so hard it hurt. Moments ago, I had been sweating, but now my tunic was soaked, and water ran down my face in rivulets, and all I could see or hear or think was that Meryn had just handed us over to the man who wanted to kill us. I watched as Meryn turned toward Talan, who—like the crowd—still appeared in shock.

"Yes," Talan said, recovering his composure. "I do, and I will, I—"

But Meryn cut him off. "Then you will prepare yourself. The priests will take you to the Druids who will make you ready for the ceremony. The sacrifice will take place where it must, at the Sacred Circle, on the morning of the solstice. I will bring the boys to you, and at the first rays of the sun, you will know."

Talan shook water out of his beard and looked at Meryn with suspicion. "Know what?"

"Truth," Meryn said.

Talan pulled his sword and pointed it at Meryn. A low gasp escaped from the crowd. "I'm tired of your tricks," he said. "They are mine to sacrifice. Those are your words."

"And they are," Meryn said, seemingly unconcerned that he had a sword pointing at him. "Go now and prepare. Tomorrow is the solstice. We will meet in the Sacred Circle at dawn." He moved forward without a glance at Talan, returned the ebony stone to the Council and came back to us.

"With me," he said, quietly but with an edge of urgency.

We left the gathering, walking straight at the crowd who, at the last second, parted, allowing us to pass. We trudged up the path that now ran like a muddy stream, and into the deserted streets which were a morass of mud.

It wasn't until we arrived at the hut that I found my voice. "What happened?" I asked.

"We've just been handed a death sentence, that's what happened," Charlie said, glaring at Meryn, "You didn't even try." I expected Meryn would be angry, but the Druid made no reaction. He simply stood silent, leaning on his staff as the rain beat down on him.

"I will tell you what happened," Meryn said. "I just took you away from a man who vowed he would not let you out of his grip." Charlie looked at the mud at

164

his feet.

"Inside now," Meryn continued. "Get out of your wet clothing, dry yourselves, eat, rest, and try to sleep. Dawn will come early, and I've much to do." Then he turned and walked away, up the muddy lane, toward the gates of the village.

"But what do we do about tomorrow?" Charlie called after him.

"Trust," the Druid said without looking back, "and have courage."

Chapter 24

Inside the hut, the fire had been lit and the air was stifling and smoky. We took the shutter off the window to get some fresh air, but the rain came in, so we blocked it off again. In the brief time we had it open, however, we saw two of Talan's warriors standing in the rain on the far side of the road. They weren't looking our way, but it was clear what they were there for. We resigned ourselves to staying in the hut, no matter how uncomfortable it was.

There was a pot of … something, hanging from a hook near the fire pit. I assumed we could heat it up if we wanted something to eat, but right now I didn't think I could eat anything without throwing it right back up. New clothes were laid out for us—tunics, undergarments, and the moccasin-type shoes the Celts wore—which was good because ours were ready for the scrap heap. We hadn't been able to change for a week, and our clothes were muddy and torn, and mine had some of Kayla's blood on it from when I was helping her.

The thought of Kayla made my stomach do another lurch. Was she alive? If so, where? There wasn't anyone to ask, so I kept silent.

"Hey, these new clothes," Charlie said. "I'm not sure I like the look of them."

They were white, with a coloured trim. Standard

tunics—thankfully, not slave garments like we currently had on—except that the fronts laced up with a strip of leather. If the leather was undone, they would open to our navels.

"Talan said he wanted to sacrifice us," Charlie said. "These look like something made just for that purpose. I'm not wearing it."

"It's clean and it smells better," I said. "And what difference will it make? If you wear what you have on now, Talan will just tear it off you. Or not."

Charlie went silent for a while. He sat on the floor in front of the fire, holding the clean tunic. I sat next to him, both of us staring into the embers.

"What do you think is going to happen?" he asked after a few minutes.

"I don't know," I said. "All I know is I'm fed up with waiting. Everywhere we've gone someone has been promising to kill us. And this is the worst; at least at the palace we got to take a bath every day."

"But do you wonder, you know, happens? Will we wake up in our bed, or will we really be, you know …"

I shrugged. "I don't know. I can't know. All I do know is Meryn said to trust him."

"Do you?"

"I don't think we have a choice."

There was nothing much to say after that. We changed into our new, sacrificial, tunics, then heated the mystery meal up and ate it with wooden spoons out of the pot, even though plates and cups had been set out for us. There was also a clay jar of the sweet wine they called mead. It was all there was to drink, so Charlie filled our cups, and we drank that. After a while, the rain let up and we were able to remove the shutter. The air that came in was fresh and cool, the

167

heat wave having been, at last, broken by the storm. Outside, Talan's warriors stayed at their post. The sky grew light as the clouds thinned, then dark, as evening approached.

We waited, but Meryn never returned. So, we waited some more. As I poured our third cup of mead, or maybe our fourth, Charlie, leaning back and, watching the fire we had built up with the few sticks of wood we had found, said, "There are things going on here that we don't understand. I think Meryn is using us to get what he wants."

"Well, that at least means keeping us alive."

Charlie nodded. "We just have to hope he knows what he's doing."

I nodded and we watched the fire in silence until it burned to embers and then, warm and dry, with stomachs full, and made drowsy by the mead, we laid on the straw mat and fell asleep. When we woke, the fire was out, the night was black and Meryn, dressed in his Druid robe, was standing over us, holding a lantern. "It is time," he said. "Rise and follow me."

I wiped the sleep from my eyes and, still groggy, rose. Meryn left the hut, and Charlie and I followed him into the night. The storm was over, but the sky remained dark. The rain had left the streets inches deep in mud, water and manure and I worried about losing my new shoes. Light rain fell as we walked through the streets and, above us, an inky sky stretched from one horizon to the other, hiding the moon, the stars, and all the heavens, behind the clouds. If not for the light from Meryn's lantern, we would have been in total darkness.

The streets were silent and empty, and we saw no one, not any of Talan's warriors or even any guards, as we passed through the opening in the inner circle. At the gates of the outer walls, the guards allowed us to pass without comment. Outside the city, we turned north and walked along a path next to a river. The path was wide and firm and, even in the pitch darkness, we had no trouble following the dim light from Meryn's lamp.

After half an hour the rain stopped completely, leaving only the light rustle of the leaves, the gurgling of the river, and the sound of our soft footfalls on the hard-packed earth.

Charlie, walking behind Meryn, asked, "Where are you taking us?"

"To the Sacred Circle," Meryn said. "It is a fair walk from here and we must be there before sunrise."

"And what happens when we get there?" I asked.

"If it pleases the gods," Meryn said after a long pause, "Talan will see the truth, the circle will be completed, and you will be free."

"And if it doesn't please them?"

There was a longer pause.

"The gods work in ways we do not always comprehend. But they have been with us thus far, I see no reason for them to desert us now."

We walked for what seemed like an hour, and then another. In the third hour, the sky turned from black to a canopy of grey and we could see trees silhouetted against the clouds, and the river became visible as a silver stream glimpsed through gaps in the bushes. Meryn extinguished his lantern and we walked on.

"How much further?" I asked, when the third hour stretched into the fourth and I felt like I was about to drop from exhaustion.

"Not far now," Meryn said. He kept his eyes

169

forward, using his staff as a walking stick, as if he was out for a Sunday stroll, but when he spoke again, his voice sounded grave. "Prepare yourselves. When we arrive, you are going to need all your courage, for I am going to ask you to do something that would weaken the knees of the bravest warriors."

"What's that?" I asked, as a feeling of dread bloomed in my stomach.

"You will look death in the face, and it is imperative that, when death looks back, you do not turn away. Keep your nerve, stare it down. It cannot hurt you."

"Are you saying we can't be killed?" Charlie asked, with a lilt of hope in his voice.

"That is not for me to decide. But you saw the Talisman, you touched it, and were touched by it. You know what has been foretold. Until that happens, death has no power over you."

That should have made me feel better, but it didn't.

"But the Talisman, when I held it, didn't tell me much," I said, "so how do I know if it's something in the future or if it already happened."

Meryn nodded. "That is the way of the Talisman. You will know the truth when it is time."

"That may be so," Charlie said, "but Fabianus is convinced the Talisman is telling him the truth, that he will be emperor. How do we know that's not the true truth?"

Meryn slowed his pace, then stopped.

"What Fabianus does not understand," he said, turning to look at us, "is that the Talisman is both a gift and a curse. For most people, the Talisman is simply a curiosity, a pretty rock polished smooth as a mirror. When they look at it, they see only their reflection. But the chosen, when they look at the Talisman, they see

170

into a world others know nothing about. For the chosen, the Talisman is not a mirror, it is a window, and to understand what you see in that window, you must understand the goddess who created it.

"Brighid is powerful, she rules the sun and the earth, the day and the night, the fire and the flood, and, like the Talisman, she has two sides. On one side, she has the face of a beautiful maiden, but the other is hideous. Those who she touches, those with a pure heart, when they look into the Talisman, they see what they need to see. Others, those whose spirits look inward, will see what they want to see; they believe it is a blessing, but it will lead them to ruin."

"But what does that mean about what we saw?" I asked. "Are our spirits good, or bad? How can we know if what we saw is true?"

"The very fact that you doubt shows your nature. A man who is convinced of his own righteousness will never doubt, and this will be his undoing. The vision the Talisman gave you, was it something you desired, something you longed for?"

Both Charlie and I shook our heads.

Meryn nodded slowly, as if satisfied by our answer. "Then you can be certain it is true."

He turned, then, and continued walking, and we followed.

We crossed a rickety wooden bridge and left the river behind, heading onto a path that led over a broad expanse of grassland. Soon after, a familiar sight appeared on the horizon.

Ahead of us, the black border where the land met the sky was broken by a structure that looked something like an immense crown made of stone. As we drew nearer, I could make out the individual uprights and thick lintels that described the concentric circles of Stonehenge.

A wall of earth surrounded the structure in a circle nearly three hundred feet across, and the outer circle of Stonehenge itself was nearly a hundred feet in diameter. It was in better condition than the last time I saw it, with only a few of the colossal stones laying on the ground, as if a giant hand had swept them aside. Inside the ring, taller uprights topped with horizontal stones stood in the shape of a horseshoe, its open end facing the brightening sky.

It was not as impressive as the coliseum, or the massive walls, of Noviomagus Regnorum, or the extravagant facade of the palace, and yet—squat and stodgy as it was—it possessed a ponderous magnificence. Its silent stones exuded a sense of permanence, making me feel like an interloper, entering a sacred place where the stones alone, which looked as if they had risen naturally from the soil, had the right to exist.

As we passed through the outer circle to the inner, Meryn said, "We have arrived. And now we must hurry, for the solstice is nearly upon us."

Chapter 25

It was nearly dawn. We had been walking for hours and both Charlie and I were tired and hungry, and I was ready to faint. My stomach felt hollow, my feet ached, and I began to wonder if that had been Meryn's plan all along, to make us too tired to put up a fight. I glanced around, looking for Talan, but saw no sign of him.

In the distance, all around the circle, mounds of earth were scattered across the plains. Closer to us stood a few wattle and daub huts. At the door of the hut nearest the circle, two figures in grey robes waited. Meryn ignored them, and instead led me and Charlie around the inner structure, the horseshoe, with its open end facing the dawn. All around, the land lay bathed in a soft, shadowless light, for the sun had not yet risen, and the eastern sky remained covered by thin clouds.

We entered the horseshoe to a familiar scene: two stone tables—last time there had been only one, and a hole in the ground where the second should have been—were in line with the edges of the horseshoe. I recalled weeds and brambles growing around the structure the last time we had been there, but now the ground was pounded flat, and only low grass grew in the outer circle and beyond.

The Altar Stone stood near the base of the

horseshoe, at the head of the tables. It was almost twice my height and about half as wide and, unlike the other stones, its surface wasn't rough, but polished and smooth as glass, its speckled face nearly sparkling. Without looking, I knew that some distance from the circle, directly in line with the horseshoe and Altar Stone, were two smaller stones arranged side by side, with a small gap between them. In the books I had read about Stonehenge, some claimed that, at dawn on midsummer's day, the rising sun shone through the gap and, when its rays hit the Altar Stone, it would glow. I had a sinking feeling that we were about to see if that was true or not.

"Come," Meryn said, "I will prepare you. Then I will bring Talan. Remember what I told you. Do not show your fear; meet his eyes, hold on to your courage."

"But what's going to happen?" I asked, my voice sounding small even to myself. "What are we supposed to do?"

"You fear what is to come," Meryn said. "That is natural. To trust transcends the natural and moves you toward the supernatural; this is how you touch the spirit world. And that is where you must go."

Charlie shook his head. "This is too much. Maybe we should just run."

I put a hand on his shoulder. "No, we have to do this. I can't explain why, I just know we do."

"You are indeed a wise man," Meryn said without turning. "But enough talk. We enter the sacred place now. It is time to be still."

Meryn led us to the tables, which were made from flat slabs of grey rock held up by thick uprights, mimicking the construction of the outer circle. On each table lay a length of rope. We climbed onto the slabs and laid down on the rough surface. Meryn went to Charlie first, perhaps because he trusted me not to run. I watched as he bound Charlie's wrist, ran the rope under the table and tied his other wrist, pulling his arms back so his chest was prominent, and he couldn't move. Then he unlaced the leather thong, exposing Charlie's white skin from the base of this throat to his waist. Charlie lay still, staring into the sky, and I wondered if he remembered laying on that table, pretending to be a human sacrifice. Back then, he had thought it funny, but he didn't look like laughing now.

Meryn tied me up and opened my tunic without a word. As he left, I raised my head as far as I could, looking toward the rising sun. I wondered if the ceremony would have to be cancelled if the sun couldn't shine, but the clouds were now parting, leaving half of the north-eastern sky a bright blue. Just our luck. Between the two distant stones the horizon glowed, and I recalled from a book I had read that one of them was called the Heel stone, and the other, the Slaughter stone, and I wished they had come up with a different name.

I lowered my head and twisted as far as I could to see the Altar stone. It was bright, but not glowing, as the sun had not risen yet.

"What if he's wrong?" Charlie asked, still staring into the sky.

"About what?"

"Everything. Anything."

I relaxed and lay, like Charlie, staring at the sky, surprising myself by how calm I felt. "I don't suppose it matters now."

"Yeah," Charlie said. "I guess you're right about

that."

He didn't say any more. I laid still, breathing in the cool morning air, listening to the sound of the distant birds, smelling the grass, feeling the hardness of the rock beneath my back. I waited, breathing slowly, remembering what the Talisman had shown me. Water. I hadn't been near any since then, so it must be in the future. My future. Meryn had been right about that. Talan wouldn't kill me. He couldn't. Not if what the Talisman had shown me was true. If. If not, then how could I stop him? I pushed that thought from my mind, breathed deep again, and waited.

Meryn returned, leading Talan, who wore a white robe. Talan's hood was down, revealing his face, painted in stripes of red and white and allowing his red hair—braided with strips of white and blue ribbons—to hang lose around his shoulders. His eyes were narrow, his lipped pressed together in a tight line; in each hand he held a stone knife. His hands, and the knives, were dripping blood.

Meryn positioned him at the foot of my table. "Remember the teachings," Meryn said to him. "You spill their blood as a gift to the gods, not to satisfy your rage; such a gift will anger them."

"Gift or no," Talan said. "Seeing their beating hearts in my hands will not fail to satisfy me."

Meryn shook his head. "You have practiced? You know what to do."

Talan looked at the dripping knives, his eyes gleaming. "Your priests were satisfied, so should you be."

"Very well, then," Meryn said. "I will leave you now; there are minutes to go. Remember, you must wait until the solstice sun ignites the Altar Stone."

176

Talan grinned. Without a word, Meryn turned and walked away. I watched him go and as the Druid stepped out of sight, I saw the sun peek above the horizon. I turned away, looking into the sky, at the grey and white clouds and the widening gaps of blue between them. Again, I felt the breeze and drew a breath, taking in the early morning scents of earth and meadow grass. The air had a crystal clarity about it, as if I could ping it, like one of mom's crystal vases, and hear it ring. Then I looked at Talan, who stared down at me, his teeth barred in his grotesquely painted face.

"Why aren't you crying," he snarled. "Why aren't you begging for mercy? Are you so weak that you let your life go without a struggle?"

I stared into his eyes and said nothing.

The tops of the towering stones that made up the inner horseshoe were now bathed in sunlight. After a few moments, the first rays of light hit the Altar Stone. I looked to the rising sun, but light stabbed at my eyes, and I turned away, straining my neck to look at the polished stone towering over us. The top half, where the rising sun struck it, glowed with reflected light.

Talan raised his arms and shook the knives at the dawn sky. "The alter stone will soon be consumed. Then the sacrifice begins."

I drew another breath and lay still, waiting.

The sun rose higher. The Altar Stone glowed.

"The time has come," Talan said, stepping between the two tables. He raised his arms, each hand holding a bloody knife, ready to strike us both at the same time.

"I spent the night practicing on lambs," he said. "Now, you are here, more lambs for me to slaughter."

He tensed, and so did I, but my mind remained clear and calm.

"Cry," Talan shouted, "beg, plead, struggle. Why do you just lie there?"

"We're not here to die," I said. "We're here to show you the truth."

I had no idea what that was supposed to mean, but it sounded like something Meryn would say, and it seemed to have the desired result. Talan hesitated again, the knives hovering above our chests, trembling in his fists.

The rising sun glowed behind Talan, and the rays reflecting from the Altar Stone shone on his face, surrounding him in light. "The moment has come," he said again, his face cut by a humourless smile. "I will have my revenge." I drew a breath. Keeping my gaze on Talan's wild eyes, trying not to look at the knives.

Then the light dimmed. Startled, I looked away from Talan, beyond him, feeling suddenly faint with disbelief. At the entrance of the horseshoe, blocking the sun's rays, stood an angel, clad in a shimmering white robe, haloed by the morning light. Charlie gasped as he saw the apparition. Talan lifted his eyes to the altar stone, staring in mute anger at the suddenly dull surface. With a snarl, he raised his arms, the knives trembling in his fists. "I will not be denied."

Then the angel spoke, in a quiet, yet commanding voice. "Grandfather," it said, "stop."

Talan stood as still as the stones that surrounded us, his eyes wide, his mouth open. Then the knives slipped from his hands, clattered onto the stone tables, and fell to the ground.

Chapter 26

Talan gasped and spun around. "Who are you?"

The angel drew back its hood. A halo of fiery red hair glowed in the rays of the rising sun.

"Kayla," Talan whispered, "have you returned from the spirit world?"

The ethereal silhouette moved forward, fading from glowing angel to the earthly form of Kayla in a white dress. "I'm not a ghost, Grandfather."

Talan fell to his knees and threw his arms around her, engulfing her in a bear hug, his big shoulders shuddering. "I thought you were lost to me. All these years I thought you dead."

"And I you," Kayla said, also sobbing. "I was taken by Fabianus, along with mother, and sent to a farm in the east."

Talan held Kayla at arm's length. "Your mother, Ameena, she lives?"

Kayla shook her head and Talan engulfed her again.

"Fabianus was going to sell us," she said, "in the Londinium markets, but these boys stopped him. And when he was going to execute me, they helped me escape. If not for them, I would be communing with the gods."

Talan pushed her away, turned his face toward the sky and let out an anguished wail as he tore the ceremonial ribbons from his hair and scrubbed at his face with his robe. "And I meant to kill them," he sobbed. "I meant to kill your saviours."

He scrambled on the ground for a moment, then stood next to my table, tears streaming down his paint-smeared face, with one of the stone knives in his hand. He stared down at me, holding the knife in front of him. "Why didn't you tell me?"

A hundred thoughts raced through my mind. We didn't know. We had also thought Kayla was dead. But then the simplest, most honest answer came, the reason Meryn had orchestrated all of this: "You wouldn't have believed us."

Talan's head dropped as he cast his eyes to the ground. "I have been a fool. The mystic is right, you are the chosen, the ones who have been sent to do what I cannot."

He cut me free then, and I felt a weight lift that I had not known was there. I held my hands in front of me, the cut ropes still dangling from my wrists, feeling as if I might float away.

Beside me, Charlie sat up, his chest heaving. He pulled the ropes from his wrists, flung them to the ground and drew a deep, shuddering breath.

Talan dropped the knife once more and, still standing, pulled Kayla to him. "All was darkness when I first laid eyes on you," he said, looking down at me. "All I could see was your spilled blood. But you have brought the light back into my life. My debt to you is boundless, as is my guilt. I pledge to serve you, and I beg your forgiveness."

I nodded. So did Charlie. There was nothing else we could do.

"Yes," I said, still staring into the sky, marvelling that I wasn't floating among the clouds. "To not forgive would mean surrendering to anger and bitterness. I see that now." I said this, not to Talan, or to Charlie or even to convince myself. The words seemed to float from me, leaving me slightly giddy and serene. Then, to my annoyance, a hand grabbed me, breaking my reverie, and I found myself engulfed, along with Charlie, in Talan's painful embrace.

"You brave, brave boys," he said. "You gave my Kayla back to me and for that I can never thank you enough." Then Kayla came and took Talan's place. "Nor I," she said.

We all left the circle then, walking into the rising sun, and found Meryn waiting for us at the outer circle, clothed in his robe, holding his staff.

"Your eyes were opened, then," Meryn said, as we approached.

"Yes," Talan replied.

"And you release the boys?"

"Humbly, and with thanks."

Meryn's hood moved as he nodded his head. "Then go now. You tread a different path to these boys."

Talan crushed us in another embrace. "I will never forget what you have done, and remember, I am forever your servant."

Then Kayla came and hugged Charlie. They embraced for a long time, and I began to feel strangely jealous. Then she came to me, and I felt her arms around me, and her strong body in my arms and I remembered how weak and sickly she was, and I almost started crying. I pulled away and brushed a hand across my face. Looking into her eyes, I saw she, too, had changed. The angry girl was gone. Standing before me, her hand still clasping mine, was a young woman, her eyes clear, bright, and determined.

"… for all you've done." I heard, and realized she had been thanking me.

I shook my head. "You've done more for us than we can repay."

Kayla nodded. "The circles have been closed."

Talan took Kayla's free hand and gently guided her away. They left together, hand-in-hand, walking across the grassy plain.

Charlie looked at me. "We're free, then?"

Meryn nodded. "So you are."

"What did she mean by the circles?" I asked when Talan and Kayla were well out of earshot.

"The circles of the universe," Meryn said, leading us away from the stones. "The stars, always in place, yet they complete a circle in their season. The moon rises, falls, follows its daily path, and its monthly phases. And you, Kayla and Talan also fell into orbit around one another, and that circuit has been completed.

"When the Roman's attacked, Talan believed Kayla and Ameena had been killed, and they believed he had been killed. That is the larger circle. When you arrived, you set in motion what culminated in Fabianus ordering Kayla sold, but you prevented that, making another circle. And in the Villa, when you put the Birch-Tar on Kayla's back, you saved her life. And now, she has saved yours, and been reunited with Talan. All the circles are now closed, but one."

I sighed. "The Talisman."

Meryn nodded. "Fabianus stole the Talisman from Talan's people, from the Land, and you—who are not from this land—will complete that circle."

"I can't believe it," Charlie said. "For the first time since we arrived, we're not someone's slave or prisoner or under the threat of death. And now we're going back

182

to the place where everyone wants us dead."

"Yes," Meryn said, "it is what you came here for."

We walked south, over the track we had come by, rejoining the river, and continuing along its banks, shaded from the sun as it rose higher in the sky. We should have been exhausted, but I felt strangely exhilarated, and Charlie didn't look like he was flagging, either.

"I expect you'll be ready for sleep before we reach the village," Meryn said when Charlie informed him of this. "But there will still be plenty of daylight after you are rested."

And so, we walked on, and the morning grew warmer and by the time we reached Sarum, we could barely keep on our feet. We were allowed into the village without question. Meryn led us to the stone hut and, without even taking off our shoes, we fell on the straw mat and drifted into sleep.

But just before nodding off, a thought suddenly struck me, and I turned to look up at Meryn. "You knew about Kayla," I said. "You had her brought to you. She was here all along. That's how you knew our names. She told you. And you knew having her back would please Talan, so why didn't you just show her to him when we got here?"

Meryn slowly removed his robe and leaned his staff against the wall. "It would not have had the same effect," he said. "Talan's grief was strong; it needed a strong remedy."

"So, it was all staged?"

Meryn, looking strangely normal in his rough pants and wool shirt, smiled. "That's how the prophecy works: part destiny, part luck, part theatre."

Chapter 27

It was early evening, though still light, when we woke. Meryn was gone, but there was food—a potful of cold stew, cheese, and some crusty bread—so we ate, sitting next to the unlit fire, and waited. The storm had broken the heat and now, though it was warm outside, the stone hut held onto the chill, making us wish we could start the fire, but having no idea how we might do that. Through the tiny window I saw inviting blue sky, but we felt it more prudent to remain where we were.

A while later, Meryn returned, carrying two sacks, and wearing a white tunic that hung to his knees, a small cloak that wrapped around his shoulders, and soft leather shoes with sturdy soles.

"Have you eaten?" he asked.

We told him we had.

"Then we must prepare and leave now. All is in place, and time grows short."

The sacks turned out to be Roman back packs, and we were supposed to carry them. On top of that, we had to put our old slave tunics on—though they had been cleaned and repaired—and lace sandals to our feet. All Meryn carried was a leather satchel draped over his shoulder, and his staff.

"The journey will be easier, and we will make better time," he said, leading us out of the hut, "if we travel the Roman roads. I will be a free citizen, and you, my slaves."

"So, we're slaves again," Charlie said, crossing his arms.

"It will keep you from having to speak to anyone, and, as slaves, no one will pay you much notice."

That satisfied me, and soon after Charlie relaxed.

The sun was already baking the mud, turning the streets of Sarum from mucky soup into a soft clay the consistency of Play-Doh. We picked our way through the lanes, out the gates, and onto a path that eventually led to a smooth stone highway.

Sarum was fading from sight before I realized we had left without saying goodbye to Kayla or Talan (though I was more concerned about Kayla), and I doubted we'd ever see them again. I thought of mentioning this to Meryn but realized there was no point. There was no going back.

The sun set shortly after we left Sarum, and before long, darkness began to fall, so we left the road and set up camp in a cluster of trees. It wasn't much of a camp, just some cleared ground with piles of leaves to sleep on. We ate some of the food we had brought with us and wrapped in the blankets we'd been carrying in our packs while Meryn made use of his cloak. The night was warm and the moon—nearly full now—shone bright, so we didn't bother starting a fire.

In the morning, we drank some water, had a light breakfast, and set out again.

Having sturdy shoes, a light pack, and a smooth surface to walk on meant we made good time. We passed other people—groups of farmers, horse carts, an occasional band of soldiers—but the road was wide enough that they didn't hinder our progress, or us

185

theirs. During the hottest part of the day, we sat in the shade near the side of the road, and Charlie and I went to find more water. When the sun cooled, we resumed walking through the afternoon and early evening, stopping occasionally to pass the water jug around. When the sun was low, Meryn called a halt and we set up camp again.

This time, he started a small fire, and we ate the rest of the food we were carrying. This started to worry me, but I saw Meryn wasn't concerned, so I put it out of my mind. When full darkness arrived, we slept.

The next day, we came to a city, and I realized why Meryn had allowed us to use all our provisions. It was still early when we passed through the city gates onto a street that led, straight as a ruler, through the centre of the town. It looked, and smelled, a lot like the city near Fabianus's villa and, like that city, it was cramped and packed with people. Though we had not been walking long, I was already tired because I hadn't eaten anything. Then Meryn stopped at a stall by the side of the lane and bought something that looked like fried dough with a sticky syrup on it. Whatever it was, it tasted great and made me feel a lot better.

It took some time getting through the city. Meryn stopped here and there, jostling into the crowds, and haggling with stallholders as he bought food that we added to our packs, and another blanket, that he put in his satchel, along with his Druid robe, which was the only other thing in it.

It was past noon by the time we left the city, which Meryn told us was called Venta Belgarum by the Romans, exiting through the western gate into the agreeably fresh air of the countryside.

We walked through the afternoon, then camped in

186

a field, where Meryn lit a fire and cooked some of the food he had bought. For the first time since we left Sarum, I went to sleep with a full stomach. The next day we walked longer, eating only dried meat and bread and, by the time we camped, there was little left, and I wondered if we were near another city.

Meryn offered no clue, but the next morning we finished the rest of the food and had only water to drink as we walked. Then, as the sun dropped low, Meryn led us off the road and into the trees.

"The villa is not far away," Meryn said. "We must now be cautious."

He led us through thickets and forests where progress was hard, and the brambles tugged at our clothing and tangled in our backpacks. Eventually, we took the packs off and, since they were empty, left them behind. Still, staying hidden meant slow going and the sun had nearly set by the time we reached the edge of the forest overlooking the villa. We hid ourselves on a rise, lying behind a cluster of bushes where we could see the palace, and the distant city.

The palace was quiet. No one was promenading on the northern portico or in the massive courtyard. All we could see were soldiers, in groups of three and four, marching around the perimeter.

The city, however, was as lively as the villa was quiet. The western gates were open, and people swarmed around a huge sprawl of tents, huts, carts, kiosks, smoking fires, haggling men, and docile horses. It looked like a makeshift city that rolled from the base of the real city walls halfway to the palace.

"The Market of the Horse Moon," Meryn said. "Full moon tonight; it will light your way, but it will also shine for your adversaries. Go carefully."

"Aren't you coming with us?" I asked.

"You are the chosen, not I," Meryn said. "And I am needed elsewhere."

"But we can't—" Charlie began.

Meryn silenced him with an upraised hand. "You can, and you will."

"How will we get in?" Charlie asked. "How will we get out?"

Meryn looked through the bushes at the palace. "There is no one better able to answer those questions than yourselves. Go, retrieve the Talisman, get your cloak, and return."

A sudden realization made me go cold. I dropped my head into my hands. "Oh no."

"What is it?" Charlie asked.

"The cloak. Kayla said she knew where it was, but she never told us."

Charlie groaned. "If we don't know where the cloak is, we'll never find it, even if we have all night."

Meryn raised himself to a crouching position. "You forget so soon," he said. "The Talisman reveals to the chosen what they need to know."

"You mean the Talisman will show us where the cloak is?" I asked, without lifting my head from my hands.

"Trust and have courage," Meryn said, his voice growing quiet. "The prophecy is about to unfold. Follow where the Talisman leads, and all will come to pass."

I heard a rustle beside me and looked up to see Charlie edging forward for a better view. "This is Deja Vue," he said.

"I fail to grasp your meaning," Meryn said, the first time I had ever heard him express confusion.

188

"This is exactly what you did to us last time," Charlie continued, staring at the latest trio of soldiers as they patrolled the north wall. "You sent us into a den of thieves—us and our friend Pendragon—to get our cloak and the Talisman. And that was impossible too."

I glanced up at Meryn, who appeared to be deep in thought.

"Did I, now?" he said, at length. "And so, we complete another circle."

"And then you disappeared on us," Charlie said, not taking his eyes off the soldiers.

Meryn remained silent for a while, then said. "And yet you are here."

"Well," I said, peering through the bushes with Charlie, "things didn't go quite as planned, but I guess it all worked out."

"That's not saying it will work out this time," Charlie said, turning to Meryn. "Hey! Where'd he go?"

I turned around. The Druid was gone.

Chapter 28

We waited as the daylight dimmed and the townspeople and market stall holders settled down for the night, until the only sounds were men talking quietly around campfires and horses stamping impatiently in the grass. The soldiers guarding the palace were also quiet, and invisible in the darkness, but their footfalls provided assurance that they were still on patrol.

Long after sunset, as the glow faded from the western sky, the moon rose, full and bright, turning the night into perpetual twilight. All the while we stayed still and quiet until, at last, we decided it was as dark as it was ever going to get. Only then did we move, low and slow and as silently as we could, through the tall grass to the bushes bordering the road. Careful to stay within the shadows, we made our way along the road to the west of the villa and waited for the soldiers we knew would soon be coming. On schedule, they appeared out of the darkness, four men marching two abreast. They passed where we were hiding and disappeared around the corner.

"Now," I whispered.

We sprinted over the road and through the low grass to the long portico of the west wing. Crouching in the shadows, we waited and listened. Nothing.

"The doors," Charlie said. "Before they come

back."

We crept to the nearest door but found it locked. We moved further along, to the next door, and found that one locked, as well.

Charlie shook his head. "It's all buttoned up. How are we supposed to get in?"

"I don't know," I said. "Try climbing one of the columns. Maybe we can get on the roof."

It seemed a good idea, but it was like trying to climb a greased pole. The polished surfaces of the stone columns were slick and the best we could do was a couple of feet before sliding back to the ground.

"It's hopeless," Charlie said.

I had to agree, but then I remembered something.

"There were temporary supporting posts holding up the roof over the outdoor pool," I said. "They'll be easier to climb, if they're still there."

We moved down the porch, heading for the pool. Then we heard people approaching.

"Quick, hide," I said.

Charlie looked around. "Where?"

The porch stretched, wide and flat, from one end of the wing to the other, its uniformity broken only by the pool and the half-finished pavilion jutting into the yard. We couldn't reach the pool in time and, even if we could, there was nothing there to hide behind. And if we ran, whoever was coming would surely hear our footsteps. Our only chance was the darkness.

"The shadows," I said. "Lay flat and stay quiet."

We crouched against the wall, squeezing into the dark areas where the moonlight didn't penetrate. Then we held our breath and waited.

"Gaius and Cato, you will guard the northwest corner."

It was Fabianus, leading a band of three soldiers, coming from the south wing.

"If they come onto the porch there is no way they won't find us," Charlie whispered. We both watched, our hearts pounding so hard I feared the sound would give us away. But when the soldiers came to the junction of the pool and the porch, Fabianus led them away from the villa, around the perimeter of the tiled patio.

"I want two guards at each corner," Fabianus continued, "watching in both directions for a full view of all areas."

The group drew level with us, just a few yards from the porch, but none of the soldiers looked our way. Still, the moonlight showed them clearly enough that I was able to recognize them: Cato and Gaius, the soldiers who had chased us into the forest, along with their leader, Captain Remus.

"The patrols have returned to their quarters," Fabianus said, "to prepare for departure. Those of you staying behind will man your posts day and night. Understood."

The soldiers replied in unison. Cato and Gaius marched to the corner while Captain Remus accompanied Fabianus around the pool, back toward the southern wall. We watched until they were out of sight, then turned toward the others. They stood together, at the end of the porch, clearly visible in the moonlight, one facing our way, the other looking along the north wall.

Minutes ticked by. We hardly dared breathe let alone speak. When one of the soldiers spoke, we both froze, certain we had been spotted, but he was merely talking to his partner.

"This is an insult," Cato said. "A Roman soldier guarding an empty dwelling; I should be marching north with the rest of the army."

"We're being punished for Captain Remus's caution," Gaius said. "If he had allowed us to chase those children, we'd be with the army now, instead of reduced to nurse maids."

Cato continued to look our way. I wished, if they were going to have a conversation that they would at least face each other.

"Granted," Gaius said after a few minutes of silence, "there may be benefit in remaining behind. Once Fabianus is gone, we can find better things to do than stand out here. The palace is most salubrious, and rumour has it that Fabianus has hidden a vast treasure inside."

Cato snorted. "Wishful thinking."

"It wouldn't hurt to look around a little," Gaius said. "We're missing out on the spoils of battle, so a little payment for our services is only right."

Cato turned to Gaius and the two of them began an earnest conversation, but with lowered voices. Then they both turned away from us and disappeared around the end of the porch. From the snatches of conversation I was able to overhear, it seemed they were speculating on what they might get away with in Fabianus's absence. But that didn't interest me. What mattered was, they could no longer see us if we moved. I motioned to Charlie. He nodded, and we began creeping along the porch toward the pool.

We checked again to make sure the guards weren't looking, then sprinted to the construction site, which looked a lot less like a construction site than the last time we had seen it. Cenacus and his crew had been

193

busy, and for a moment I was afraid that all the work had been completed. Moonlight glinted off the water in the pool and the decorative tiles on the patio were all in place. The convenient openings in the wall were, naturally, finished and closed off but, to my relief, a few of the supporting posts were still in place. Being made of wood, they were slimmer than the stone columns and a lot less slippery. I wrapped my arms and legs around the nearest one and began to shimmy up. Charlie went to the next one and did the same.

Climbing silently was difficult. The rough wood scratched my arms, legs, and face, but the roughness made it easy to grip and I was soon at the roof edge. I pulled myself up and lay on the tiles, panting as quietly as I could. A few seconds later, Charlie was beside me.

Silently, we made our way along the roof of the new pavilion to the main building, where the gap with the porch was now nearly closed. The join was seamless and, in the dim light at least, it was impossible to tell where the old terracotta tiles ended, and the new ones began. There was a small, unfinished section that I assumed Cenacus's crew were planning to continue working on because the scents of smoke and Birch Tar rose from below as we looked through the hole. Frustratingly, we couldn't get in that way; the spaces between the beams were too narrow, and even if we could squeeze through, we'd land in the pool, and that would make too much noise.

We moved on, climbing from the porch onto the main building, where we scaled to the peak and then descended to the porch roof overlooking the internal gardens. It was the middle of the night, and the house was empty, so no one would be walking in the gardens or relaxing on the porches, but that didn't mean there wouldn't be soldiers keeping watch. We waited awhile but saw and heard nothing. Finally, with no other option, we jumped.

The muffled thuds as we hit the ground were magnified by the silence of the night. We both lay on the dew-covered grass, listening for sounds of alarm.

"I think it's safe," Charlie said after a few moments.

We tried the door leading to the pool, but it was locked, as was the next one, and the next one.

"We're trapped in here," Charlie said. "What's going to happen if we can't get out?"

I looked around at the huge garden and expansive porches and realized everything had been shut up. Charlie was right. If we couldn't get into the villa, we'd not only fail to get our cloak and the Talisman, but we'd also be spotted as soon as it got light.

"Wait," I said. "There's one door we haven't tried."

We went to the north portico and felt along the wall, searching for the seam in the panel that Kayla had used. After a few minutes of frantic searching, I felt it. Together, Charlie and I eased the secret door open.

The small hallway was dark, and turned pitch black when we pulled the door shut behind us. We had to feel our way, which wasn't difficult in such a small space, but then we came to an intersection.

"Which way?" I whispered.

"I don't know," Charlie whispered back. "I just followed Kayla. She knew the way. Don't you remember?"

I tried to think back, but it was no use. I had no idea.

"This way," I said, trying to sound confident.

We moved on, feeling along the rough walls, and soon came to a door. Carefully, slowly, we pushed it open.

The room was large, dimly lit by moonlight streaming through the high windows, and—as near as I could tell—empty. We slipped silently into the room. It smelled faintly of smoke and cooked meat. There were long tables in the centre of the room and counters along the edges where pots and crockery were neatly stacked.

"The kitchen," Charlie said.

I nodded. "Seems to be. And if that's the case, the dining rooms will be nearby, and Fabianus's apartment won't be far away."

This was encouraging. In our searching of the villa, we'd been to the kitchen, so, even in the dark, we could find our way from here. The oak tables were no longer cluttered with clay pots and baking pans, and no carcasses hung from the hooks along the walls like the last time we had seen it, so it wasn't hard to feel our way through the gloom without bumping into anything. We entered the hall and made our way to the dining rooms. Then we turned down the corridor we had been barred from searching during our stay—the corridor that led to Fabianus's rooms.

The corridor looked empty, but as soon as we entered, a light flared, and voices came out of the darkness.

We froze. Then two men appeared, stepping out of a door midway down the corridor. They weren't raising an alarm, so they hadn't seen us. Not yet. Silently, we stepped backward, to the main hall, then sprinted to the first doorway, which led to a private dining room.

We waited, listening, hoping whoever it was didn't come our way. Yellow light danced in the hallway as the men drew closer.

"…the remaining slaves will keep to their quarters when not working."

"Yes, sir."

It was Fabianus, talking to Captain Remus

"Your soldiers will stand guard in pairs, four hours on, four off, seven days a week …"

The voices grew fainter and the light dimmer as they walked away.

"… do not keep the same two men together. Keep switching them. I don't want them plotting …"

We waited until the hallway was dark and quiet. Then we waited some more.

When we were sure the hallway was empty, we peered out of the dining room.

"No one there," Charlie said. "Let's go."

We went back to the corridor, walking as swiftly and silently as we could. It was darker than the main hallway, but I recognized the double sized, arched entryway to Fabianus's rooms. It led to a reception area, and the bedchamber beyond. The reception room was now empty, and although the bed, with the oaken chest at its foot, still dominated the bedroom, the rest of the furnishings were either missing or pushed into one corner. Even the wall coverings and tapestries were gone; the only decoration that remained was the marble bust, still sitting in its niche, on the far side of the room.

My heart began to pound, fearing Fabianus had already packed the Talisman away. We rushed to the adjoining room. Relieved to find the dresser still there. Charlie pulled the top drawer open.

"It's here," he said in an excited whisper. "At least the box is. And look what else I found,"

For a moment I thought he meant our cloak, but

the drawer was far too small. Instead, he pulled out a leather bag.

"It's my money," he said, showing me the "C" embossed on the bag. "I'm taking it."

"But we gave him our money," I said. "It isn't ours. Put it back."

He ignored me and dipped into the drawer again. "And what's this?"

He pulled out a folded piece of parchment. Shaking it open, we looked at it, trying to decipher the strange markings in the dim light.

"I think it's his map," I said. "The one he made while we were burying his money."

"Should we take this too?" he asked. "Or at least rip it up? It would serve him right."

I wanted to tell him to put them both back. They weren't ours and it wasn't right, but I felt strangely reluctant to say it.

"Keep the money," I said, "but put the map back. And get the box."

To my surprise, he didn't argue, and instead dropped the map back into the drawer and fastened the bag onto his belt. Then he pulled out the puzzle box and shook it. A thumping from within confirmed it was not empty.

"Open it," I said.

Charlie pushed on the sides of the small box, then pulled, then twisted. "I can't. Kayla just opened it; she didn't show us how."

I reached out for it. "Let me try."

I took the box and shook it, pushed its sides one at a time, pulled on it. Nothing worked.

"Put it on the floor," Charlie said.
"Why?"

"Just do it."

I set the box down and Charlie stomped on it.

"Ow!"

"Quiet!"

"But that hurt."

We stood, silently looking down at the little wooden box. Fear and frustration threatened to overcome me. We needed the box open. We needed the Talisman to tell us where our cloak was. Then Charlie grabbed the box and ran back into the main room.

"Follow me," he said. "I have an idea."

When I caught up with him, he had already set the box on the bedroom floor and was trying to lift the marble bust and not having much luck.

"Help me," he said.

I got a grip on the bust and together, though with difficultly, we lifted it.

"Hold it over the box," Charlie said.

Awkwardly, we shuffled a few steps to where the box was and tried to hold the bust over it.

"Ready," Charlie said. "One, two, three."

We jumped back as the bust landed on the box, with a thud that reverberated through the room, then thumped to the floor. The bust's nose and right ear broke off, but when we looked at the box, it was barely scratched.

"That had to alert everyone in the palace," I said. "Quick, drop it again."

We hauled the bust off the floor and raised it as high as we could. This time, the box cracked. Charlie knelt on the floor, smashing the box against the base of the fallen bust until it broke, and the Talisman rolled out. I snatched it up and, sitting cross-legged on the tiles, looked into it.

"What do you see?" Charlie asked.

"Nothing yet."

I stared at the black surface, a dark hole in the dim light. Soon my head began to swim as it began pulling me in, making me feel like I was falling. In the distance, I saw a room. The image came closer, and grew clearer. It was the same room we were in. I could see us, standing by the far wall. And someone else was in the room with us.

I pulled myself away, my breath coming is short gasps. Charlie looked at me, his eyes wide. "Do you know where our cloak is?"

"Yes," I said, getting to my feet and pulling Charlie up with me. "Fabianus is wearing it, and he's coming this way."

We ran toward the reception room, and the exit to the corridor, but after a few steps we skidded to a halt. Fabianus was standing in the doorway, with a sword in his hand.

Chapter 29

Fabianus stepped forward. "So, the thieves have returned."

"We're not thieves," I said. I noticed him glancing toward the other room, where the bureau was. "Your treasure map is where you left it. We only came for the Talisman and our cloak. Unlike you, we don't take what doesn't belong to us."

Fabianus glanced again toward the room. "Strangely, I believe you speak the truth. Those are fine words from someone about to lose his head." He charged forward but we dodged him, bounded over the bed, and rushed for the door. But Fabianus was quicker. He cut us off and we found ourselves backing into the corner, hemmed in by the bed and Fabianus, who continued to edge nearer. Charlie stepped back, bumping into me. I fell against the wall and my hand brushed against a seam. Hoping Fabianus couldn't see what I was doing, I fumbled with the panel, pulling on the edge of the door.

"I shall be rid of you two at last," Fabianus said, taking another step, "and my treasure will be truly safe."

"You forget about the third," I said. "Kayla knows."

"Kayla is dead."

"No, she's alive," I said, working my fingers deeper into the seam, "and she's a Celt."

"What's that to me?"

"A Celt can come up behind a man and slit his throat before he even realizes he's there."

Fabianus smiled. "Nice try. If you thought that little—"

"NOW KAYLA!"

Startled, Fabianus whirled around, his sword brandished against an enemy who wasn't there. I pulled the door open, grabbed Charlie and yanked him inside with me.

"Run," I shouted, slamming the door.

"How?" Charlie asked. "It's pitch black."

"Do the best you can."

We jogged through the tunnel, our hands brushing the wall to keep us on track. By the time we reached the other end we could hear Fabianus coming up behind. We took one turn, and then another, and then burst into the kitchen.

"It's not the outdoors," Charlie said, "but at least we know where we are."

We shoved one of the oak tables against the door. It wouldn't stop Fabianus, but it would slow him down. Seconds later, as we were running for the main hallway, we heard him pounding on the door.

The North hallway was quiet and dark. We raced down the corridor, not caring how much noise we made, praying it would remain empty long enough for us to reach the grand entrance hall. Then the darkness gave way to flickering lights as a dozen soldiers, wielding swords, and carrying torches, charged toward us.

I slid to a stop and turned around, rushing back the way we had come, with Charlie right behind me. The hallway remained empty of soldiers, and Fabianus, and we ran as fast as we could. Still, by the time we turned the corner into the western wing, they were almost upon us.

We ran toward the construction site, hoping the mini-obstacle course would slow them down. But they continued to gain on us, and Charlie began to fall behind.

"Hurry," I said.

"The money bag keeps bouncing around. I can't run as fast."

"Get rid of it, then."

He yanked it from his belt and threw it behind him. The bag opened and the coins, winking gold and silver in the torchlight, bounced and rolled across the floor. The soldiers in front saw them, and dove to the floor, scrabbling to scoop them up. The soldiers behind them either tripped, or joined the melee, fighting for the coins. Swords and torches skidded toward us as men brawled on the tiles and the orderly pursuit turned into a chaotic tangle of men, weapons, and fire.

"C'mon," I shouted.

"No, wait," Charlie said. "This is … it's what the Talisman showed me. The fire. Over here, help me."

To my shock and horror, he ran toward the soldiers, but then he put his shoulder to one of the big stone cauldrons.

"Hurry," he said. "It's heavy."

I ran to join him, pushing with my back, using my legs as pistons. Slowly, the big vat tipped, then tumbled, splashing liquid tar over the floor. Then, with a whoosh that took my breath away, the hall burst into flames. Soldiers screamed, swords clattered, feet pounded. Most of the soldiers ran away, but some tried to get through the flames.

"That's the fire I saw," Charlie said, his eyes bright with excitement. He looked around quickly. "Over here."

We ran to another pot, straining and groaning, pushing until it, too, spilled its contents. Another breath-taking whoosh, more screams, and no soldiers.

Flames licked up the freshly varnished walls, into the rafters, turning the hallway into a tunnel of fire, roaring toward us. I stared in disbelief, unable to move.

"Come on," Charlie said, grabbing my arm.

We ran around the pool, to the double doors opening onto the formal gardens. They were barred shut, but from the inside. Charlie lifted the wooden bar, and I pulled the doors open. Outside, on the portico, Fabianus was rushing toward us. We slammed the doors and slid the bar home, feeling it jolt as Fabianus smashed against it.

The air grew smoky and hot, and the flames came closer. High above, the thick green glass covering the windows exploded like rifle fire, sending sharp reports careening down the hallway. With more air, the fire roared with sudden intensity, and its forward pace quickened.

"The south hall," I said. "Maybe we can get out through the bathhouse."

We ran on, our eyes stinging, our throats burning. Toward the end of the corridor, the air became cooler and the smoke thinner, and as we turned the corner to the south hallway, we felt we were finally out of danger. But there, less than a hundred feet in front of us, was another band of soldiers. As soon as they saw us, they charged, their swords and torches waving above their heads. We spun around and ran back toward the fire.

"We can't go this way," Charlie said, his voice

rasping.

"Well, we can't go that way, either."

We ran, nearly blind, gasping, and wheezing, while behind us the soldier's cries grew more distant and less enthusiastic. I couldn't see, but I felt we must be inside the fire. Flames crackled all around and, most ominously, above us, and the tiled floor felt hot even through my leather shoes. To go much further would mean burning to death.

"We've got to go back," Charlie said.

"No," I said, shouting above the noise. "There's something here, something the Talisman showed me. Keep going."

"But we'll—"

The floor disappeared from beneath my feet, and I fell, face first, into cool water. I floundered for a few moments, conscious of Charlie sputtering next to me, then found my feet and stood, with the water coming up to my chest. "It's the pool," I said. "We're safe."

The inferno raged around us. The double doors were ablaze. I felt lightheaded and unable to breathe. Then I heard a new sound, a zip followed by a splash and a hiss of steam. It began slowly, one every few seconds, then increased in frequency and intensity. I looked around; the surface of the pool was pock-marked by small splashes and plumes of steam.

"The lead," Charlie said. "It's melting and dripping through the roof. This whole wing is about to collapse."

The fire raged on all sides of the pool now. There was no chance of escape. Behind us, the double doors boomed and bowed as soldiers slammed it with a battering ram. We didn't have much time. If we didn't roast to death, Fabianus would kill us. But my mind remained calm. I thought back to the vision, to what the Talisman had shown me. "The conduit," I said. "The tunnel at the deep end. It leads to the outdoor pool. Swim for it."

Charlie took a breath and swam for the bottom.

I hesitated, replaying the vision, remembering the feeling of being surrounded by water, stuck, unable to move, drowning. It was a feeling I would do anything to avoid experiencing again. But I couldn't stay there. I drew a tentative breath, and hesitated.

Then the double doors burst apart in a shower of burning shards, and Fabianus leapt through the gaping hole. I took another breath and, this time, went under.

The cacophony of shouting soldiers, roaring fire, and steaming water suddenly fell into silence. All I could hear was the sound of my pounding heart. I kicked and worked my arms, dimly aware that I was still clutching the Talisman. I put everything out of my mind except swimming for the tunnel, focusing solely on getting through it. It didn't seem far when I had seen it that day with Cenacus, but by the time I reached the bottom of the deep end, my chest was burning.

I found the tunnel and scrambled inside, pulling myself along, my eyes on the light at the other end. Moments later, I was there. Above me, I saw moonlight and reflections of the fire. I kicked for the surface, but then jerked to a stop. I looked back to see what had happened. Had my foot got caught somehow? But all I saw was the grinning face of Fabianus, our cloak floating around him, his hand gripping my ankle.

I kicked with my free foot and struggled but couldn't break free. My lungs were bursting, the pain unbearable. I thrashed, panicked, desperate to hold my breath but knowing I couldn't.

Suddenly, arms encircled my chest, and a sharp pull freed my foot. Hands propelled me upward. I surface, sputtering and coughing, and swam for the shallow end.

A few seconds later, Charlie came up, splashing and shouting. He seemed to be struggling. I grabbed him and pulled him toward me and together we staggered up the incline to the tiled patio that surrounded the pool. Behind us, the night was ablaze.

"You okay?" Charlie asked.

I nodded and coughed up more water. Then I noticed he was holding something. Something big.

"The cloak?"

Charlie nodded, grinning. "I managed to pull it off him."

I sat hard on the tiles, my breath still ragged. "Then we have all we came for," I said, between gasps.

Charlie sat, holding the sodden cloak in his lap. The roar of the fire was deafening, and the heat too intense to stay where we were. The entire wing was now engulfed and, although there were soldiers rushing around, none of them paid any attention to us.

"We need to go," Charlie said.

I ran my hand over the cloak, still not believing it was safely back with us. Then I looked at the Talisman, clutched in my other hand, its dark surface reflecting the inferno. "Yes," I said. "Let's go."

Then Fabianus bobbed to the surface.

Chapter 30

Charlie started to run. I wanted to but couldn't. Fabianus thrashed his arms, then slipped beneath the surface. He wasn't coming after us, he was drowning and, even though he was who he was, to leave him like that felt wrong. I laid the Talisman on the tiles and waded into the water.

What are you doing?" Charlie called.

"He's drowning," I said. "We've got to help him."

Charlie stopped running. "You're kidding."

I didn't wait to see if he was coming or not. I splashed into the pool, heading to where I had last seen Fabianus go under. When the water hit my shoulders, I took a breath and ducked under. In the dim light I saw a dark shape against the lighter tiles of the pool bottom. I swam for it and grabbed an arm.

Fabianus was heavy, weighed down by his armour. I tugged but couldn't move him very far. Then I sensed someone beside me. Charlie grabbed Fabianus's other arm and together we pulled. I remembered the lifesaving techniques I read in First Aid manuals, but we didn't try any of them. We just dragged his limp body along the ramp leading to the edge of the patio. Soon, my head was above water. I gulped air and pulled harder. Together, Charlie and I dragged Fabianus into shallow water, trying to keep his head above the surface, even though he didn't appear to be breathing.

Once we were in water only a few inches deep, Fabianus got heavier, and we struggled to move him. Inch by inch we heaved his body onto the patio where he lay limp and unresponsive.

"Turn him around," I said. "With his head going downhill."

Charlie grabbed his legs, I took his arms and together we pivoted the body until Fabianus lay, face down on the tiles, his head pointing down the slope that led to the pool. I looked at his face, which was waxy and pale. The frenzied glow of the fire reflected in his open, unseeing eyes, and water trickled from his blue lips. I wasn't going to give him mouth-to-mouth, but I remembered something I had read about drowning victims that had more appeal. I jumped and landed on my knees on Fabianus's shoulder blades. Water gushed from his mouth and nose. When I got up, I heard his lungs gurgle as they filled with air. I jumped again, and again water spewed out, but not as much. When I got up that time, Fabianus coughed and drew a ragged breath.

I jumped back, startled and amazed, as Fabianus struggled to his hands and knees, convulsing, and vomiting up water and bile. He heaved and retched and slowly his gasping subsided, and he inhaled deeply, bringing colour to his pale face and blue lips.

Still shaking, he pushed himself into a sitting position, hacked and heaved some more, then slowly climbed to his feet. "You saved me," he said, his voice rasping and hushed. "You are truly noble and brave." Then he pulled a dagger from his belt. "But very foolish."

He was so close, and I was so taken by surprise, that I had no chance of getting out of his reach. Then

Charlie, instead of backing up, charged forward, ramming Fabianus head-first at his beltline. If Charlie had tried that at any other time, he would have bounced off and Fabianus wouldn't have even felt it. But Fabianus was still unsteady, so he tumbled backward as the dagger's point whizzed past my nose. They fell into the shallow water, Fabianus on his back, thrashing and cursing, with Charlie on top trying to get away.

I jumped again, this time on Fabianus's leg. He let out a howl and Charlie climbed off him, scuttling out of the pool, leaving Fabianus splashing in the shallow water.

"Go!"

He grabbed the cloak. I scooped up the Talisman and together we ran into the night, fully illuminated by the light of the raging fire. We thought we were free and clear, but as we got near the road, I looked over my shoulder and saw Fabianus coming after us.

"Unbelievable," Charlie said. "Isn't he ever going to give up?"

"He wants us too badly."

"Well, I wish he'd want something else for a change."

I stopped.

Charlie ran a few more paces, then stopped and turned. "What are you doing?"

"Hold on," I said. "I have an idea."

Charlie looked sceptical. I hoped what I had in mind worked because Fabianus, even with his unsteady gait, was gaining on us surprisingly fast. As he got close, I pointed toward the burning villa. The western wing was fully in flames now, as was half the southern wing. And now the northern wing, where Fabianus's rooms

210

were, had begun to burn. "Look."

Fabianus slowed but didn't look back. "You will not fool me a second time."

I pointed again. "Your treasure map," I shouted, "it's in your room. It's about to be burned up and then you will never be able to find it."

This time, Fabianus did look. He stopped where he was, staring in mounting panic, looking at us, the growing inferno, and back to us again.

"He's got to choose the map," Charlie said. "He can always come after us, but once the map is gone …"

But Fabianus seemed frozen, unable to accept that he couldn't have both, that he had been denied total victory.

Then Captain Remus, Cato and Gaius came from the west lawn at a full run.

"Fabianus, we need more men to fight the fire," Captain Remus called. "It is out of control."

Fabianus smiled malevolently at us, then turned to his soldiers.

"I don't like this," I said.

Charlie started backing away. "We've got to run before they see us."

"It's bright as daylight," I said. "If we run, they're sure to see us. Hide."

We scrambled to a clump of bushes near the side of the road and waited, watching as Fabianus called to Captain Remus. "You told me those boys were dead. I should kill you where you stand, you lying curs."

Captain Remus stopped. Cato and Gaius stood behind him.

"We thought they were," Remus said. "On my life, I swear."

Fabianus shambled close to Remus. "I will have

your life if you do not kill them this time," he said, shouting into Remus's face. "And bring me the items they have stolen, or I will have you flayed alive."

Remus looked toward the road, scanning left and right. "Where are they?"

Fabianus glanced over his shoulder, then turned back to Remus. "They were there seconds ago. They cannot be far. Find them. Kill them."

"Yes, Fabianus," Remus replied.

"Bring their heads to me within the hour and I will reward you with two month's salary. All of you."

"Thank you, Fabianus."

"Don't thank me!" Fabianus said, already heading for the flaming North Wing. "Kill them!"

"Fabianus, stop," Cato called when it became clear he meant to enter the burning villa. "It's too dangerous." He started toward Fabianus, but Captain Remus restrained him.

"You know nothing," Fabianus called. "I have seen my future, and it does not end here. Find those boys."

Rushing forward, he jumped through a burning gap that had once been a doorway while the soldiers, and Charlie and I, watched in disbelief. Moments later the roof collapsed, sending an explosion of flames hundreds of feet into the night sky. The force from the inferno made the soldiers crouch and shield their eyes. The heat rolled over us like a blast from a furnace, bringing hunks of flaming wood with it, and making me glad for what little protection the bushes provided.

"Fabianus is dead," Captain Remus said, when the flames died down to their normal roar, "but his last orders still hold. You heard him, six month's salary for the boys."

We peered through the bushes, watching the

soldiers run directly toward us, as if they knew we were there. I heard Charlie moan, and had to summon all my strength to remain still. Even if they didn't know where we were hiding, they were about to trip over us. But if we moved, they would spot us for sure.

Then the three of them looked around and slowed their pace.

"Where are they?" Cato asked.

"They would have run to the forest again," Remus said. "This way."

They changed course, charging past us, no more than ten feet from where we lay, drawing their swords as they crossed the road and headed for the trees.

"Keep your wits about you," Remus said, as we watched their backs getting further and further away.

Charlie jumped up, bundling the wet cloak into a ball as he ran. "Come on."

I followed, climbing onto the road, and racing toward the city, away from the villa, the forest, and the soldiers.

Behind us, another section of the villa collapsed, sending flames and sparks into the air, and casting yellow light as far as the city walls. I turned, feeling heat from the fire even from that distance. The road behind us was empty.

"I think we lost them," Charlie said.

We continued on, not running, just jogging, heading toward the mass of people now streaming out of the city gates and clustering at the edges of the market. Once we got lost in the crowds, we would be home free. Then, mixed with the roaring of the fire and the growing rumble of the crowd, I heard a shout.

"There they are!"

I looked behind. In the field, halfway between the

213

forest and the road, and clearly visible in the firelight, Captain Remus, Cato, and Gaius were charging toward us.

Chapter 31

"Run!"

The road was broad and flat, and we had a lengthy head start, but the cloak—wet, heavy, and awkward to carry—slowed Charlie down. He tried to bundle it better as he ran, but it unfurled and I stepped on a trailing edge, which sent me tumbling headlong to the road. I skidded painfully over the paving stones and rolled into the bushes. Charlie rushed up beside me, still trying to gather up the cloak.

"Get up!"

I thrashed in the bushes, squirming my way out, ignoring my cuts, bruises, and skinned knees. Once free I jumped to the road, ready to run. Then I flexed my hands. Both were empty.

"I've lost the Talisman!"

I crawled back into the bushes. Charlie dropped the cloak and helped. Together we scrabbled around, feeling through the weeds, brushing aside leaves.

"Hurry, they're getting closer."

"It's got to be here somewhere!"

The sound of pounding feet got louder. They were on the road now. Charlie grabbed the cloak and got ready to run. "It's no use! We have to go, now!"

I stepped back from the bushes, my hair dishevelled, my arms skinned and pricked in a dozen places. "We have to find it."

"There's no time."

Then, from within the bush, I saw a glint of reflected moonlight.

"There it is!"

I scrambled for the light, thrust my hand through the brush and grasped the Talisman.

"Got it, let's go!"

We raced down the road, with the soldiers close behind and gaining.

The city was close, but they would catch us before we reached it. Closer to us was the crowd of curious onlookers at the edge of the market, but we wouldn't be able to get to them before Remus and his men got to us, either. The gap was too wide. If only they were more curious, they would have stood closer. Then I had an idea.

"This way," I said.

Charlie followed me as I left the road and ran toward the crowd of onlookers. Remus and his men followed. When we got close, and the soldiers were nearly upon us, I called to the crowd.

"I have a messaged from Fabianus," I said, panting, running, and shouting at the same time. "He has promised …"

I turned to Charlie. "What's a lot of money in Roman coins?"

"I don't know!"

"… a LOT of money to anyone who helps him fight the fire. But you must go now. Hurry!"

With shouts and cheers, the crowd of farmers and stallholders surged forward. We dodged between them, but the soldiers were hindered, then pushed back, by the surging throng. We ran into the temporary settlement, zigzagging among the tents, carts, and livestock. Behind us, we heard the soldiers enter the camp.

"Split up," Captain Remus said. "Out flank them. I'll drive them forward."

We moved from tent to cart to tent, keeping as quiet as we could, trying to stay hidden. Behind us, Remus and his men moved with frightening efficiency, slicing through tents, kicking over stalls, looking under wagons. Ahead of us rose the walls of the city.

"They're cutting us off," Charlie said, "and we've got nowhere to go."

I tried to think. Hiding would do no good. We couldn't run left, or right, and our way would soon be blocked by the wall.

I started to slow down. "It's no use," I said. "We're trapped."

Then, from the darkness ahead of us, I heard a voice. "Mitch, Charlie, this way, quick!"

We ran forward, toward another camp where a man stood next to a cart loaded with turnips. Behind the cart were two horses, tethered next to a small tent. As we drew closer, I realized the man was Lucius.

"In the tent," he said. "Stay quiet."

We dove through the tent flaps and lay in the darkness, holding the cloak over our faces to muffle our panting. Outside, Remus and his men raged through the camp, coming closer.

"You there," Captain Remus shouted, so close it made me jump, "account for yourself; why are you not fighting the fire?"

"I stayed behind to guard my belongings," Lucius said. "And a good thing, it seems. Two ruffians came by moments ago; I am certain they would have stolen all they could carry if I hadn't seen them off."

"Where did they go?"

"They ran south, back toward the road."

"This way," Remus called. "Follow me."

Then silence returned to the camp. I expected Lucius to come to the tent, but he remained outside, so we stayed in the dark, waiting, listening. Outside, the cart creaked, and then I heard the horses snuffling and pawing the ground. After a few minutes, Lucius spoke from just outside the tent. "Into the cart as quick as you can."

We slipped out of the tent, ran to the cart, and jumped onto the pile of turnips, surprised to find they were not piled up anymore. Instead, there was a hole, like a shallow grave, in the middle of the cart.

"Lie down," Lucius said.

We crammed into the hole and Lucius piled turnips on top of us until we thought we would suffocate.

"Keep still," he said. Then he climbed onto the driver's bench, clicked his tongue softly, and the horses began to move. The cart jerked and swayed and rumbled across the field. Then I felt a bump as we mounted the paving stones.

The clip-clop rhythm of the horse's hooves increased as we headed down the road. I felt a change in the rumble of the wheels as we entered the city through the Western Gate. It was night, and many people were away, fighting the fire, so the cart kept a steady rhythm as we headed toward the Eastern Gate. Our tight, dark hiding place, smelling of damp earth, and the gentle sway of the cart, nearly lulled me to sleep. Then a sudden stop jolted me awake.

"Hold," came a gruff voice. "State your business."

"I am Lucius, slave of Fabianus, overseer of his farm."

"You are his slave no more," said another voice. "Fabianus has died in the fire. Why are you on the road this time of night?"

"The tragedy has ruined the market," Lucius said. "I have sold little of my produce here, so I am going to try my luck closer to home."

"You chance travel in the night?" the gruff voice asked. "That seems unlikely."

"The gods will protect me," Lucius said.

"And that unlikelier still," the other voice said.

Then silence, heavy with suspicion.

"My turnips," Lucius said, "will go to waste if I cannot sell them in the local markets. Please take some for yourselves, as many as you wish; it would be a shame to let them rot."

More silence, then I felt the load of turnips above me lighten as the guards scooped them up. They took more and more until I was afraid they would dig us up. One next to my eye lifted away, giving me a clear view of two Roman soldiers, laden with armloads of turnips.

"You may pass," the gruff soldier said. The cart jerked again, and I heard the comforting clop of hooves.

"Be wary of bandits," the other guard called.

I watched as the cart passed under the Eastern gate and the night sky, bright with the Horse Moon, came into view. I could just make out the upper half of Lucius, sitting on the driver's bench, as we rolled into the countryside. He didn't turn, he didn't speak. Charlie and I kept still.

When we were far from the city, Lucius, still facing forward, spoke.

"Stay hidden," he said. "I want to be far gone from the walls of Noviomagus Regnorum before you show yourselves. Perhaps when we reach—"

The cart jerked to a stop.

"Remain still," Lucius whispered. "Celts."

The horses whinnied, and I heard a scuffle and a grunt, and Lucius disappeared.

"What have we here," a voice said. "A Roman? With a cart of goods stolen from our land?"

"I'm a farmer," Lucius said, his voice strained.

"A Roman farmer! Kill him. Take the horses and the cart."

I didn't have time to think. I jumped up—rising from the turnips like a zombie from a grave—and scrambled to the driver's bench.

"Do not harm that man!"

The Celts froze, surprised by the explosion of turnips and my sudden appearance. There were seven of them—three holding the horses, three holding Lucius and one standing in front of Lucius with a knife to his throat—and they all looked up at me. I thought there might be another one, sneaking up behind me, but it was only Charlie who appeared at my side, holding the cloak. Then the Celt with the knife began to laugh.

"What is this?" he jeered. "Roman slave children who think they command us? They will make fine captives."

"We are neither Romans nor slaves," I said, hoping my voice didn't sound as shaky as I felt. I held up my hand. The Talisman glowed in the moonlight. "We are the Guardians of the Talisman."

"We are the ones foretold," Charlie said, "who return that which has been taken."

The Celts stopped laughing and gazed at the Talisman. One by one the Celts holding Lucius let go and stepped away. The Celt wielding the knife lowered his hand and returned the blade to its sheath. "You? Guardians of the Talisman?" His voice contained an edge of awe, but the jeer was not completely buried. "You attempt to deceive us." He stepped forward and stretched out his hand. "Give it to me; I will be judge of its worth."

I knew I shouldn't, and that I wouldn't, but the Celt didn't look like he'd appreciate that response, so I continued to hold the Talisman up, out of his reach, and said nothing. The others didn't attack us, but they didn't let Lucius go, either, and their leader kept his hand out, waiting. I wondered how long the stand-off would last before they decided to kill us.

Then, through the silence, came the thudding of horse hooves. I looked across the plain and saw, in the moonlight, the shadows of a dozen horses heading our way. The Celts looked, too, grabbing for their weapons, but as the riders galloped closer their confidence returned and the leader turned his gaze back to me and Charlie.

The horses, carrying a dozen Celt warriors, thundered onto the road, surrounding the cart and the Celt band. They settled their horses and sat, saying nothing. The Celt leader ignored them, waved his arm impatiently and shouted at me.

"Give it. Now."

"No," I said, looking at the outer circle of Celt warriors. When I spoke again, it was them I addressed, not the leader of the Celt band. "Take us to the Druid Meryn. He will tell us who it must be returned to."

"You haven't far to look, then," came a voice from beyond the encircling horses. "And it appears I have arrived just in time." The warriors moved aside, opening the circle to allow Meryn, in his white robe and carrying his staff, and Talan—bare-chested, tattooed and wearing a jewelled sword—to pass through. They walked their horses up to the cart, edging the Celt band, and their leader, aside. Behind them, riding a black horse and dressed in a shimmering white robe, was Kayla.

Chapter 32

Meryn dismounted, then helped Kayla down from her horse, while Talan looked around at his warriors, and the Celt band.

"The Talisman has returned to the Land," he said. "And so long as it remains, the Land will be safe."

Kayla came to the cart and climbed onto the driver's bench. There was hardly room for the three of us and I worried that the spell would be broken if one of us fell, but she managed to stand between me and Charlie without knocking either of us off. Meryn stood close and looked up at me.

"Give her the Talisman," he said.

Kayla looked radiant in the moonlight, and a warmth spread through me as I placed the Talisman in her hand. We held it together, not touching, but connected. The dark pupils of her eyes, black as the Talisman, held my gaze and I felt myself falling into them, tumbling through the ages, forward through time, to where I belonged. I pulled myself back, blinking, surprised to find myself still in Roman Britain, standing on a turnip cart with a Druid Priestess. I didn't feel homesick, though. I felt I was home.

Kayla smiled and, leaning forward, kissed me on the cheek. Then she turned to Charlie and kissed him. A bit longer, it seemed to me.

"The circle has been completed," Meryn said, his arms raised, addressing the small crowd. "The time of the Romans is ending. The Land belongs to us now."

We all stepped down from the cart. Charlie and I stood with Meryn, while Kayla went to Lucius, whose eyes went wide when he looked at her.

"Kayla?" he asked. "Is that you?"

Kayla hugged him as Talan looked on suspiciously.

"He's her step-father," I said, looking up at Talan.

"If Ameena is this man's wife," Talan said, dismounting, "then he is my son."

Talan went to Lucius, hugging him and Kayla together.

When they parted, and Kayla mounted her horse, she looked down at Lucius. "Tell mother I am with my people," she said. "I am where I belong."

Lucius nodded. "She will understand."

Kayla, Talan, and his warriors rode away then, leaving us, Lucius and Meryn behind with the Celt band.

"The prophecy has been fulfilled," Meryn said, turning to address all of us. Then he looked at me and Charlie. "You have the cloak?"

Charlie nodded. "It's in the back of the cart. With the turnips."

"Then travel on, for your task is complete."

He then turned to the Celts. "These are important people. You will keep them safe on their journey."

The Celts nodded, grinning, and disappeared into the darkness.

We climbed onto the cart. Lucius sat on the driver's bench while Charlie and I climbed into the back.

"No," Lucius said. "You ride up front with me."

We rode away then, leaving Meryn behind and the

224

Celt band somewhere unseen, even though the countryside was well-lit by the moon.

The horses trotted on, making good time until we came to the forest, where it became pitch black. It was here, with the horses treading carefully through the gloom, that I was most glad for the Celts who, though invisible, were surely close by looking out for us.

By the time we emerged from the forest, the sky was beginning to lighten. When dawn broke, the Celts reappeared to bid us safe travel. Then they returned to the forest while we plodded onward, gaining speed as the day brightened.

The sun was high when we reached the farm. Ameena came to greet us, giving Lucius a firm hug as he explained, in brief, excited sentences, what had happened.

"Then Kayla is where she belongs," Ameena said, coming to us. She hugged me, then Charlie, thanking us for keeping our promise.

Titus and Cassius came to tend the horses and the cart, while Ameena led us into the villa. Despite being desperately tired, we put off sleep in favour of a soothing bath to wash away the grime and sooth our aches. After our bath, we dressed in fresh tunics and retrieved our cloak, which Ameena had washed and hung out to dry in the courtyard.

"You are brave and noble boys," Lucius said, coming up behind us. "Twice you saved my life, even though I meant to enslave you."

Charlie and I turned to face him. "You saved us too," I said, "so I guess we're even."

Lucius looked away, shuffling his feet. "You honour me," he said.

After a few awkward moments, he continued. "I am

a free man now, overseer of this profitable farm. I would be even more honoured if you would stay on, not as slaves, but as my sons, to work with me and inherit this land when I retire."

Then it was our turn to look away and shuffle our feet, searching for something to say. To our relief, Ameena came into the courtyard, a bundle of clothes in her hands, and stood beside Lucius.

"These boys won't be staying," she said softly, a hint of sadness in her voice. Then she looked at us. "You are eager to return to your own home, and your own mother, aren't you?"

I nodded, not sure if I could trust my voice. I noticed Charlie didn't say anything, either.

Then Ameena held out the bundle. It was the clothes we had arrived in. "Take these. I saved them for you. Put them on before you travel."

We went into the old bathhouse, our former prison, and changed—me into my normal clothes and Charlie into his pyjamas—and walked with Lucius and Ameena out of the farmyard, following the tracks and farm roads to the orchard where we had appeared.

"We'll just go through here, if you don't mind," I said. "It's the way we came."

"As you wish," Ameena said. "I will accompany you a little farther. Lucius, you should return to the villa for rest. You look about to fall down."

Before any of us could object, she ushered me and Charlie into the orchard, leaving Lucius behind.

Charlie, holding the cloak, led the way, searching through the trees until he found the one with the X mark on its trunk. I caught up with him and we both stood beneath the boughs, looking self-consciously at Ameena.

"Um, we're kinda tired," I said. "Is it all right if we take a nap? Under this tree?"

Ameena smiled. "That will be perfectly acceptable."

"You don't have to stick around," Charlie said. "You probably want to get back to the villa."

"Lie down," Ameena said, "and don't worry. I was a Druid Priestess. I know the prophecy, I held the Talisman, I knew of your coming, and I know you are leaving. May I have the honour of witnessing your departure?"

Charlie looked at me. I shrugged.

"Yeah, I suppose," Charlie said.

We laid under the tree, feeling the cool grass, the warm breeze, and the hot sun winking at us through the branches. Then Ameena covered us with the cloak.

"Sleep well," she said.

I closed my eyes and fell, almost immediately, to sleep.

Chapter 33
July 2014

I opened my eyes. It seemed as if no time had passed and, for a moment, I felt like I was still in the orchard. Then I saw that it was dark.

Carefully, I eased the cloak aside. Charlie was beside me, in his Star Wars pyjamas, deeply asleep. We were in his room, lit only by the full moon shining through his window. Quietly, and careful not to wake Charlie, I got off the bed, pulling the cloak with me, and tiptoed across the room to the door. I pulled it open, wincing as it creaked. No one stirred. I slipped out and went to my room, my heart pounding.

The clock on my nightstand read 3:24, just nine minutes since I left. The box was still on my bed, open from the back. Quickly, but quietly, I stuffed the cloak in, shut the box and put it back on the shelf. I decided to attach the hinges later. I was too afraid I'd fumble the screws in the dark and I was becoming terrified that Mom would hear me and get up.

With the cloak in the box and the box back where it belonged, I got under the covers, clothes, shoes, and all, and pretended to be asleep, Seconds later, I heard a door open. Footsteps in the hall came close, and then my door opened a crack as Mom peered in. She entered, walking silently across the room while I struggled to keep still and breathe slowly. She must have hovered over me, watching, for a minute or two, then she checked the box, tugging on the lock to make sure it was secure. My heart leapt, thinking that the cover would come off with the hinges unattached, but nothing happened. Then she left, and I heard her check on Charlie. Only then did she return to her own room. I didn't want to chance her hearing, so I went to sleep, wearing my clothes.

◆

When I woke up, the sun had risen, and I saw blue sky through my bedroom window. I quickly undressed, then dressed in my pyjamas and went downstairs.

Dad was still in bed, Mom was in the kitchen, and Charlie was on the living room couch, dressed in his pyjamas, eating a bowl of Rice Krispies. Across the room, the television was tuned to a morning news program, but Charlie wasn't watching it. He glared at me when I came into the room.

I sat down next to him, but not too close. "You remember, then?"

"It was a dream," he said, "but you took me against my will, wearing this." He held his arms apart, indicating his pyjamas.

"You can't be angry with me for a dream you had," I said. "But you can if you believe it was real."

"I'll be angry if I want, and you know as well as I do that it was just a stupid dream."

"Fine," I said.

"And, just like any dream," he said, taking another spoonful of cereal, "you'll soon forget it."

I didn't answer that. We both knew it was true. Just like last year, the memory would fade. I could already feel it starting to dissolve—the fear, the fatigue, the heat, the smell, the touch of Kayla's hand.

I sighed and got up, intending to go to the kitchen for breakfast, but then the sports segment on the news program ended and a human-interest story began. I ignored it until I heard the word, "England." Then I stopped in mid-stride and went back to the sofa.

On the television screen, the news reporter—a tall man wearing a raincoat and green boots—was standing in a clump of trees next to a hole and small pile of dirt. The sky was overcast, and it looked windy, but the news reporter, ignoring the weather, looked into the camera as he spoke to his microphone.

"… and this is the ordinary looking copse where it happened," the reporter said, in a strangely accented voice. "Experts are calling this the most significant find, ever. Its value has yet to be determined. We are here today with Timothy Stokes, the owner of the farm where the Roman hoard was found, and his brother-in-law, Alan Hughes, who found the treasure." He thrust the microphone toward one of the men who came into view. "Alan, how did it feel when you made the discovery?"

Alan, wearing mud-splattered trousers and a canvas jacket, smiled broadly for the camera. "It was just … unbelievable. Like something out of a dream. I was showing Tim here how to use the metal detector—we weren't looking for nothing, just playing around with it. I'd come down for a visit with the family and I'd brought my metal detector along like I always do, even though Claire, that's my wife, always complains that I spend more time with it than with her." He chuckled then, but no one joined in, so he continued. "But I wanted to try it out because I'd just upgraded from the Ace 250 model to the new Euro Ace and Tim was curious about what it could do so we come out on this field and scanned around and suddenly it starts beeping and …"

The reporter moved slowly away from the men and looked into the camera. "The size of the find, though significant, is not the most important aspect, however, is it Jim?"

The scene then shifted to the interior of a room where a man and woman stood next to a counter cluttered with microscopes, magnifying glasses, bits of broken pottery and a leather sack.

Now Charlie sat up, staring at it.

"No, Dave, not at all," Jim said. "I'm here with Doctor Winslow of the London Museum of Natural History. What is it about this find that makes it so extraordinary?"

Doctor Winslow, wearing rubber gloves and a white lab coat, picked up the bag.

"That's our coin bag," I said, pointing at the screen.

"This Roman coin purse, found inside the clay pot, is remarkably well-preserved," the Doctor said. Charlie looked at the television and the close-up of the leather bag.

"The tanning process to make this leather, as well as the laces stitching it together," Winslow continued, "are remarkably modern. It suggests the Romans were far more advanced in the manufacture of leather than previously thought. It's a very exciting find because it changes everything we thought we knew about Roman leatherworking."

"Charlie," I said, "that's the treasure we buried, that's our coin bag. It was inside, remember?"

"That can't …" He shook his head. "It's just a coincidence."

Then Doctor Winslow turned the bag around. "And we theorize this particular bag was designed to hold one-thousand denarii due to the Roman numeral M embossed on it."

Charlie picked up the remote and turned the television off.

"What do you think of that?" I asked him.

He took another mouthful of cereal.

"I think I'm really mad at you now."

Historical Note

The villa referred to in this book is modelled on the Fishbourne Roman Palace near Chichester in West Sussex. The palace, as it appears in the story, is rather grander than the actual villa, though the construction and fire are based in history.

There was, indeed, a major construction project being undertaken in the North Wing around the year 270 AD, and a fire did destroy much of the villa around that time. We don't know for certain why or how the fire started.

Now we do.

And if aficionados of the Roman era in Britain read these pages, and subsequently wish to inform me of details I have supposedly mis-represented, I have only this to say:

The boys went back in time, and this is what they saw.

About the Author

Michael Harling is originally from upstate New York. He moved to Britain in 2002 and currently lives in Sussex.

Lindenwald Press
Sussex, United Kingdom

Printed in Great Britain
by Amazon